W9-AFV-530

"I'm talking about your mistresses!"

Janine pulled away, staring up at the tanned face in the moonlight. "I have it on good authority that you keep three of them! I don't intend to become the fourth."

Nikolai released her finally. Only now was he beginning to take her seriously. "Janine, what do you expect me to say? I enjoy women as much as the next man, but you're talking nonsense." Then he was smiling again, reaching for her. "I want you, Janine. You and I are going to be lovers. You know that as well as I. Come on," he coaxed, "let's not play games. Let's go to a hotel— somewhere warm and luxurious where we can make love...."

Janine's last vestige of control slipped and she slapped him—hard....

Books by Claudia Jameson

HARLEQUIN PRESENTS
690—GENTLE PERSUASION
712—FOR PRACTICAL REASONS
737—DAWN OF A NEW DAY
777—THE FRENCHMAN'S KISS

HARLEQUIN ROMANCE
2523—LESSON IN LOVE
2565—THE MELTING HEART
2594—YOURS...FAITHFULLY

These books may be available at your local bookseller.

Don't miss any of our special offers. Write to us at the
following address for information on our newest releases.

Harlequin Reader Service
P.O. Box 52040, Phoenix, AZ 85072-2040
Canadian address: P.O. Box 2800, Postal Station A,
5170 Yonge St., Willowdale, Ont. M2N 6J3

CLAUDIA JAMESON

the frenchman's kiss

Harlequin Books

TORONTO • NEW YORK • LONDON
AMSTERDAM • PARIS • SYDNEY • HAMBURG
STOCKHOLM • ATHENS • TOKYO • MILAN

Harlequin Presents first edition April 1985
ISBN 0-373-10777-3

Original hardcover edition published in 1984
by Mills & Boon Limited

Copyright © 1984 by Claudia Jameson. All rights reserved.
Philippine copyright 1984. Australian copyright 1984.
Except for use in any review, the reproduction or utilization of
this work in whole or in part in any form by any electronic,
mechanical or other means, now known or hereafter invented,
including xerography, photocopying and recording, or in any
information storage or retrieval system, is forbidden without
the permission of the publisher, Harlequin Enterprises Limited,
225 Duncan Mill Road, Don Mills, Ontario, Canada M3B 3K9.

All the characters in this book have no existence outside the
imagination of the author and have no relation whatsoever to
anyone bearing the same name or names. They are not even
distantly inspired by any individual known or unknown to the
author, and all the incidents are pure invention.

The Harlequin trademarks, consisting of the words
HARLEQUIN PRESENTS and the portrayal of a Harlequin,
are trademarks of Harlequin Enterprises Limited and are
registered in the Canada Trade Marks Office; the portrayal
of a Harlequin is registered in the United States Patent
and Trademark Office.

Printed in U.S.A.

CHAPTER ONE

JANINE's mother slowly replaced the telephone receiver. 'There's still no answer,' she said anxiously. 'Something's wrong. Something's wrong, I just know it!'

Unperturbed, Janine Curtis gave her mother a reassuring smile, glancing quickly at her father as she spoke. He didn't seem alarmed, either. 'Don't jump to conclusions, Mum. Robbie's probably out with this girl he met recently. You saw how he raved about her in his letter.'

'No.' Her mother was adamant. 'Something's *wrong*, I tell you.'

'Rose, your tea's going cold. Come and sit down.' Archie Curtis gestured towards an armchair. 'And stop worrying, dear. Jan's probably right, if Robbie is still seeing this girl he wrote about——'

'He will be,' Janine put in, 'if he meant what he said in his letter!'

They had all been surprised, impressed, by the letter from Robbie, Janine's elder brother, not least because he was the world's worst letter-writer and it had to be something really newsworthy which would make him put pen to paper. He rang home regularly, though. Every week, in fact. Except this week. When Robbie's regular Sunday call was not forthcoming, his mother had phoned him at his apartment in Paris, but there had been no reply. Since then, over the past three days, she had tried to contact her son several times, at different times, and was now panicking because there was still no answer.

Cherchez la femme, Janine thought. She wasn't in the least concerned. Her brother was Head Chef in one of the finest restaurants in Paris; he was twenty-nine years old, had worked in several countries since leaving their home in the Channel Islands, and he was perfectly capable of looking after himself. But Robbie was a diabetic, and it was for this reason that Rose Curtis worried about her son in spite of his age.

'Perhaps he had some time off work,' Janine's father was saying. 'Maybe he's left Paris for a few days. You know, gone out of town for a long week-end.'

'Archie, it's Wednesday. That would make it a very long week-end! Besides, he told me he hasn't got any time off until New Year. Then he's coming home for a week, remember?' Rose paused, thoughtful. 'I'll ring him at work tonight.'

Archie tapped his pipe against the ashtray on the arm of his chair. 'He won't like that. You know what he's always said—don't ring me at work. He'll be cross.'

'Too bad.' She got to her feet.

Janine picked up the morning newspaper. She and her father had only got home from work half an hour earlier and she hadn't had a chance to read the paper yet. She worked in her father's travel agency in St Helier, and although it was October, when the island of Jersey had far fewer visitors than it did during the summer months, they had had an unusually busy day with people booking excursions. She was only half-listening to what was being said now, thinking it better to keep out of the discussion about Robbie.

'He won't be there yet, Rose,' her father was saying. 'It's too early. Give it an hour or so.'

'I know it's too early,' Rose said mildly. 'I'm only going to ask directory enquiries for the restaurant's phone number. Then I'll start dinner and ring him when we've eaten, all right?'

'All right, dear. As you wish.'

Janine glanced up from the paper, smiling inwardly. How dear they were, these two people whom she knew so well! Her mother was really worried, trying not to show quite how much, and her father thought his wife was being silly, but he wouldn't say so. They had been married over thirty years and not once in her twenty-three years had Janine heard them rowing. If they did fight, they did it in private.

Her father was not easily ruffled, and it was him Janine took after. At least, she liked to think so. She liked to think that like him, she was practical, level-headed and cool. Physically she was like her mother inasmuch as she was slim and she had clear, green eyes. When Rose had been younger she had had dark blonde hair, the exact colour Janine's was now. These days it was more grey than blonde, but it always looked chic, rolled into a French pleat with never a hair out of place. Her mother dressed well, too, with a great deal of flair, and this was another way in which Janine took after her.

Both her parents had been born in Jersey, and though they had travelled extensively they had never lived anywhere else. Rose's mother had been French, a petite, excitable woman whom Janine had adored. The Curtises, all of them, spoke French as well as they spoke English—which wasn't unusual for people living in the Channel Islands. But the three Curtis children had spoken French before they had spoken English.

Janine had left home at eighteen to go and work in Switzerland and had returned to the Channel Islands only a year ago, to settle down and work for her father. She adored the big old house the family lived in, she liked the island very much, but she couldn't honestly say she felt settled, even though she had been home twelve months now.

She put the newspaper down, unable to concentrate, and took a glass of sherry into the kitchen for her mother. She and her father had a gin and tonic before dinner, and they refrained from mentioning Robbie's name because they did not share Rose's alarm. They were both convinced that a woman was at the bottom of the mystery of Robbie's whereabouts. Maybe he had been sleeping at his girl-friend's place for the past few nights?

Robbie's letter had arrived in the middle of the previous week. It was addressed to Janine, although its contents were not intended for her eyes only. In fact he had ended the letter with, 'Tell the folks!' Janine had let her parents read it for themselves, had enjoyed the look of surprise on their faces when they did so.

It was a surprise Janine had shared. Never before had

she known her brother rave about anything other than his work as a chef. Robbie was not easily impressed by anything, really. Except, perhaps, a new recipe! He had certainly never before gone on about a woman the way he had gone on about Lara. Lara. He hadn't mentioned her surname, what she did for a living or what she looked like—except to say she was the prettiest thing on earth. Indeed the letter had been brief, covering only one side of the single sheet it was written on. But it had been dramatic, beginning with, 'I'm in love! I've met the most wonderful, sensitive girl it has ever been my privilege to know.' And then Robbie had mentioned her sense of humour, her intelligence and lively personality—and that was it, except for 'Tell the folks!'

There had been very few women in Robbie's life and certainly no serious or lasting relationship in his past. Had there been, Janine would have known about it, because although she and her brother saw one another infrequently, they were very close. This woman was different; Janine could feel it in her bones. Robbie simply was not the type of man who would think himself in love unless it was real. Furthermore, he had actually put it into words. On paper. And in a letter to his family, too. It was as if he had been bursting to tell what had happened to him. But he would not have told his family unless he were serious. Of course, he had made no mention of Lara's feelings in the matter, and he had obviously known her only a short time, so Janine was not jumping to any conclusions.

When her mother telephoned Robbie at work, however, Janine's speculations about her brother's love affair were forgotten. Something was, indeed, wrong. Very wrong.

Rose's face blanched slightly as she put the phone down, her eyes clouded with worry as she turned to look at her husband.

'What is it?' Archie was on his feet, moving towards her. 'Is Robbie ill, is that it? Is it something to do with his diabetes?'

'No, no, it's nothing like that. He isn't ill. At least, nothing was said about his being ill.' The colour returned quickly to Rose's face and she looked more bewildered now than anything else. 'Robbie isn't working at the restaurant any more. He's been sacked!'

'Sacked?' Janine couldn't believe her ears.

'Robbie? *Sacked?*' Archie was incredulous.

Janine was on her feet now, agitated and at a loss to understand. 'But what reason did they give? I just can't believe it!'

Her mother held up a hand. 'I didn't ask for a reason, I was so taken aback. I got through to the switchboard and they said they'd put me through to the manager. He was curt; he said simply that Robert had been sacked and he hadn't been near the restaurant for several days.' She looked from her husband to her daughter, shrugging. 'It seems there are some of Robbie's belongings in the staff locker room which he hasn't been back to collect.'

The three of them were silent for a while, each thinking their own thoughts. Janine was telling herself that Robbie couldn't be contacted because he was probably out looking for another job. But it just didn't ring true. A chef of Robbie's experience and calibre wouldn't need to spend much time looking for work. Most especially in Paris.

She was worried now; there was no denying it. Had this happened to someone—anyone—other than Robbie, there would have been little cause for alarm. There was nothing particularly unusual about people being sacked. But her brother was twenty-nine years old and this had never happened to him before. On the contrary, he was always highly thought of wherever he worked. He was by no means the archetypal, temperamental chef. Robbie got on with everyone and anyone. He was a listener rather than a talker, he had a dry, subtle sense of humour and above all else he was sensitive and fair in his dealings with people. Janine could not imagine what had brought this about.

'Janine, I want you to go to Paris first thing in the morning.' Her mother's voice was firm, but her anxiety showed through.

Janine wasn't about to argue, she was anxious

herself. 'Of course.' She looked at her father. 'I'll take the morning flight, Dad. There shouldn't be any problem.'

'I'll get a seat reserved for you now.' Archie's face was impassive, but that was the way he was. Always calm and controlled. He reached for the phone. With his contacts it would be easy to book a seat, even at such short notice.

Janine went to her room and packed an overnight case. Then she found a medium sized case and shifted her belongings into that one, unsure why she was doing this. After putting the small case back into her wardrobe, she stood by her bedroom window, pondering as she looked down at the dark shadows which was the garden at the back of the house. Maybe Robbie would need a little moral support? Perhaps he'd like her company for a few days? When she found him, that was.

Paris was familiar, chilly but as exciting as ever. Janine knew the city well; it was a short plane journey from the island where she had been brought up and she had been here countless times in the past—shopping with her mother, mainly.

It was a little after eleven when she settled into the back seat of a taxi and gave Robbie's address. Going firstly to his apartment was the obvious thing to do, even though she wasn't expecting to find him at home. Robbie had only lived in this particular apartment for four months, and Janine hadn't been there before. It was quite central, which meant it was quite expensive, and according to her brother it was small but comfortable.

The concierge might know of Robbie's whereabouts. Failing that, she would talk to his neighbours, and if that failed she would go on to the restaurant and speak to some of his colleagues. Someone had to know where he was.

It was an old building. Old but in good repair. Janine looked up at it as she paid the taxi driver, wondering which floor her brother lived on.

'Monsieur Curtis's apartment is on the first floor. At the back.' The concierge, who was female, nodded towards a flight of stairs. She was openly curious, and Janine smiled at her.

'I'm Monsieur Curtis's sister. I believe he's been away for a few days . . .'

The concierge shrugged expansively as Janine was about to ask whether he had left an address or a telephone number. 'I wouldn't know, *mademoiselle*. I have also been away for a few days—I came back on duty this morning. But I saw your brother when he came in about an hour ago. He's in his apartment now.'

Janine blinked in surprise and then laughed delightedly. Robbie was at home? What luck! She thanked the concierge and headed for the stairs, aware that the other woman was thinking her a little strange.

She paused for a moment before knocking at Robbie's door, feeling suddenly foolish. Her brother might not be pleased by this visit; it could be interpreted as interference. She shrugged resignedly. Robbie knew how Rose worried over her children—all three of them. She always had and she always would, no matter how old they were!

'Who is it?' Robbie's voice came through the closed door. It sounded guarded, suspicious.

'It's me! Janine.'

'Janine?' The voice was disbelieving now, astonished. 'Jan!'

As her brother flung the door open, Janine's breath caught in her throat. He had a badly bruised eye; it was black and blue and yellowing around the edges. The skin on his cheekbone had been cut slightly, and the whole thing looked awful. 'Good God, what's happened——' Her voice trailed off as she saw the bandage around his wrist. Then she became aware of someone standing in the doorway behind him.

'Jan!' Robbie flung his arms around her, obviously delighted that she was there. 'Oh, it's so good to see you! Come in, come in! Let me take that case. No, no, it's okay,' he smiled, 'there's nothing wrong with my other wrist!'

Janine was filled with a mixture of relief, curiosity and worry. Robbie's brightness was false, and it just wasn't like him to be so demonstrative.

There followed a rather strange few minutes as Robbie ushered her into his living room and introduced her to the other person.

'Lara.' He slipped an arm around the girl's shoulders. 'Lara, this is my sister, Janine. Jan, this is my fiancée, Lara Nekrassova.'

The girl's surname, which certainly was not French, came as yet another surprise among many. His *fiancée*? A dozen thoughts and as many questions tumbled through Janine's mind as she took the hand the girl was offering. Lara's handshake was vigorous, warm. 'So you're Robert's sister! Oh, I'm so pleased you're here!' She spoke in English which was only slightly, and delightfully, accented.

The welcome was so warm, so sincere, that Janine couldn't help feeling flattered. She said nothing which would indicate that she knew about Lara—not wishing to embarrass her brother—and she tried hard not to show her surprise.

Lara was so *young*! She was also as pretty as Robbie had said she was. She had a mop of black, curly hair, pale skin which had a natural blush on her cheeks and positive blue eyes framed by lashes as black as her hair. She was shorter than Janine, and despite her jeans and baggy sweater, and a little excess weight, there was something doll-like about her. Janine warmed to her immediately, aware that Robbie was watching both of them closely.

'Robbie, Lara, what—what's happened?' She gestured towards her brother's face, his wrist, but everyone had started talking at once and it was minutes before she discovered the reason for Robbie's black eye.

'But you're beautiful!' Lara was saying. She reached out to touch Janine's hair which was falling in soft curls around the shoulders of her jacket. She looked so serious that Janine couldn't help laughing. 'And your hair—it is what the English call honey blonde, isn't it?'

'Actually, no.' The older girl laughed aloud. 'It's a little too dark for that.'

Robbie, who had been saying something about making coffee, slipped an arm around Lara's waist. 'Lara is very outspoken, Jan. She says what she's thinking, as you'll discover for yourself.'

'I already have.' She watched the pair of them as they smiled at each other. Yes, the feeling was mutual. Lara was as much in love with Robbie as he was with her. She smiled inwardly, touched by what she was seeing. She felt almost like an intruder. 'Robbie, I'm sorry to drop in on you without warning, but Mum has been trying to ring you since last Sunday. She's been worried—you know how she is. Then last night she tried to ring you at the restaurant and was told you weren't working there any more, and the reason. So she asked me to come and——'

'And find out what was happening,' Robbie finished. He nodded and sighed, long and hard.

'It's all my fault——' Lara began.

'It's nobody's fault, darling.'

Janine could stand it no longer. 'You've been in an accident, Robbie. Please tell me what happened.'

'It wasn't an accident!' Lara said vehemently. 'It was deliberate! Robbie's been in a fight, and it's all my fault! I told Nikolai that I missed my period last week, that I might well be pregnant!'

Janine just stared at her. Lara's remark—all of this—was so unexpected that she didn't know what to say next. Pregnant? A fight? And who was Nikolai? 'A fight?' she managed, her eyes trailing over Robbie's bruised face. 'You? In a fight? Robbie, none of this is making any sense at all! Will you please start from the beginning?' She was determined not to be alarmed. There had to be a reasonable explanation for this—all of it. She sank into an armchair as Robbie asked Lara to make the coffee.

Robbie sat facing her, not knowing where to start. He ran his fingers through his light brown hair. His tallish frame was hunched slightly in an attitude of tension. Considering he was a chef par excellence, Robbie was slim and slightly built. But it was his diabetes which dictated his eating habits, and in any

case he was one of those people who never put on
weight.

Janine waited patiently, giving him time to order his
thoughts. Whatever had happened was still a source of
worry to him; that much was obvious. 'How long are
you staying?' he asked suddenly, glancing at the case
which he had dropped near the sofa.

'A day, a few days.' Janine shrugged. 'Whatever you
like.'

'What did they tell Mum, at the restaurant?'

'She was put through to the manager. He told her
simply that you'd been sacked. That's all we know.
Robbie, where have you been for the past few days?'

'In Lille—at Lara's home. That is, we were at her
home on Sunday and then we spent a few nights in a
hotel about twenty miles away. We wanted to keep . . .'
He looked his sister directly in the eyes. 'Jan, Lara and I
are going to be married.'

Janine nodded, smiling. 'I'd gathered that much!
You've got it bad—the pair of you. But she seems very
young, Robbie.'

Whether the remark irritated or disappointed him,
she couldn't be sure. He got to his feet suddenly and
moved around restlessly. 'Sorry if I said the wrong
thing. Hey, I am pleased about this,' she said. 'Very
pleased.'

'It's okay.' Robbie managed a smile. 'She's young,
Jan. She's eighteen.'

Janine said nothing. She had thought Lara even
younger. 'I take it Nikolai is her father? You've met
with opposition, is that what's wrong?'

'That's putting it mildly! No, he isn't her father.
Nikolai is Lara's brother.' Unconsciously, his fingers
brushed over the bruise on his face, and he smiled
wryly. 'Her big brother.'

'*He* did that to you?' A wave of anger rushed through
her. 'Her brother did it? But what business is it of his if
Lara wants to get married? I mean, all right, I can
see——' She broke off, remembering what Lara had
said. 'Is she pregnant, Robbie? I don't understand . . . I
thought you'd only just met her!'

'I have. Well, just over three weeks ago. A couple of weeks before I wrote to you about her. You did get my letter, didn't you?'

Janine remained patient. She smiled goodnaturedly. 'Yes. And you're still not making much sense, you know. I still don't understand what's been going on. What's all this got to do with you being sacked? And why is Lara's brother against the marriage? And what sort of a name is that, Nikolai Neb—Neb . . . What is it again?'

'Nekrassov. Nekrassova is the feminine version of the name. Does the name mean anything to you?'

'Not a thing. It isn't French.'

'It's Russian. Nikolai and Lara were born in France, but they're of Russian descent. Their father lived all his life in France but was born in Russia. He was brought here as a babe in arms during the Russian Revolution in 1917.'

Janine's eyebrows rose. 'Oh!'

'Nikolai is a lot older than Lara,' Robbie went on. 'He's almost twice her age, in fact. He's thirty-five.'

'And he's very much the head of the family.' Janine said it first, nodding slowly as she began to understand. 'The parents are dead, right? And Nikolai's word is law?'

Robbie was impressed by her deduction but not in the least amused. 'You've got it in a nutshell. He's her official guardian, and her only relative.'

When Lara came in with the coffee, the pair of them told Janine the story from the beginning. She listened with rapt attention, interested but sharing none of their anxieties. There was a solution to every problem, that was her way of thinking. Something could be worked out.

Lara was a new student at the Sorbonne. She had been there only since the start of the academic year, and on telling Janine this, she said also that she had never wanted to attend the university—any university—in the first place. 'It was my brother's idea. I started there at his insistence—he thinks education is very important. But I don't dislike it there. I would have stayed on, just

to please him, if he had been reasonable about my
marrying Robert.' She pointed to Robbie's face, her
eyes flashing angrily. 'But after this, I'm not prepared
to do *anything* to please him! I'm dropping out! I shall
do it officially next week. I'm going to——'

'Keep to the point, darling,' Robbie said patiently.
'Tell Janine how we met, to begin with.'

Robbie's initial brightness had long since faded,
but Lara remained almost passionate in everything she
said. Janine thought her quite lovely in a youthful,
effervescent sort of way. 'It was just over three weeks
ago, at the end of September. A girl friend of mine
was having a dinner, a birthday dinner, in the
restaurant——'

'The restaurant where Robbie worked?'

'Yes. There were ten of us in all. All females.' Her
blue eyes sparkled as she flashed them at Robbie.
'Anyway, the meal was so good that my friend asked to
see the chef, she wanted to thank him personally.
Voilà!' She waved an arm towards Robbie, the gesture
typically French. 'We looked at each other—and that is
all. Two days later we bumped into each other, and I
mean that literally, on the Champs Elysées. We
remembered each other, of course, and Robert asked
me if I had time for a cup of coffee. That was the
beginning!' She said it proudly, as if it were an item of
world-shattering news. 'It was difficult at first, with
Robert at work during the evening and me at school
during the day, but we spent every minute we could
together. Now we are lovers and we have long and
beautiful nights together. Soon we will be married.'

Janine glanced at her brother, unable to keep the
amusement and surprise from showing in her eyes. Lara
was indeed outspoken! She cleared her throat. 'I . . . see.
And when do you hope to be married?'

'We'd planned on doing it at New Year, when I had
time off work.' Robbie answered.

Lara was sitting on the floor by his chair. She
reached for his hand and glanced at Janine almost
defiantly. 'But now we don't have to wait so long.
Robert has no job, no commitments. We are free.'

'Yes, you're free,' Janine said quietly, deliberately. She had to make it clear to Lara that there was no need to look defiant or defensive where she was concerned. 'Nobody can stop you from doing as you wish, Lara, and I personally wouldn't even try to do that. I'm sure Robert's parents wouldn't interfere, either. Nevertheless, things are not straightforward, are they? Tell me what your brother said, and why he objects.'

Lara was quiet for a moment. Suddenly she slipped into her native French, her eyes bright with tears. 'Nikolai can go to hell! I'm sick of him trying to control my life!'

Robbie took over then. 'Jan, I'd better explain that Nikolai owns the restaurant where I worked. I didn't know it when I first asked Lara out. I didn't even know the owner's name, incredible though it may seem. Neither did the rest of the kitchen staff. He has very little to do with the running of the place. He calls in occasionally and talks to the manager. I'd seen him once, coming out of the manager's office, but I had no idea of his name and I didn't know Lara was related to him. I'm telling you this because for one thing, Nikolai seems to think I'm some kind of fortune-hunter.' He broke off, sighing.

'Go on.' Janine kept an impassive face, but she saw that things were more complicated than they had at first appeared.

'Nikolai is a very rich man. He——'

'He's also power-mad!' Lara cut in, bitterly.

'He owns several properties in Paris,' Robbie continued. 'Luckily, he doesn't own this building, otherwise I'd have been thrown out of my home as well as my job.' He laughed hollowly. 'Anyhow, after I'd been seeing Lara for a couple of weeks, I wrote to you about her. Lara knows this. And she wrote to Nikolai about me. We were both ... sort of preparing our families for what was to come. You see, Jan, what's happened to Lara and me is very difficult to explain ...'

'We started to love each other right from the beginning.' Lara's effervescence had vanished. She was

speaking quietly and very seriously, her eyes appealing
to Janine for understanding. 'Obviously, we are aware
of the difference in our ages, but it is irrelevant to us.
Our backgrounds are very different, and that doesn't
matter either. I see how this thing looks to Nikolai, and
to you too, perhaps. We have known each other a very
short time, but it is real, Janine. I love Robert and I
want to be married to him.'

Nobody spoke for a moment. Janine continued to
look at Lara, beginning to appreciate that she was not
as immature as she had at first thought. But of course
she wasn't. If Robbie had fallen in love with her, there
must be a great deal more to her than the first
impression had shown. She thought of the letter Robbie
had written, of the intelligence and sensitivity he had
spoken of.

Robbie continued with their story. 'When Nikolai got
Lara's letter, he phoned her and invited us to visit him
in Lille last Sunday. As it happens, Lara was going to
ring him and tell him to expect us in any case. We
planned on telling Nikolai about the wedding first.
Then we were going to ring Mum and Dad and tell
them.

'We'd anticipated objections from Lara's brother. We
knew he would say she was too young to marry. But we
thought we would overcome his objections.' Robbie's
face tightened as he drew in a long breath. 'We drove to
Lille in time for lunch. The first hour or so passed
pleasantly enough, with Nikolai being fairly easy to get
on with, almost companionable——'

'Until he told him we were going to be married,'
Lara put in.

'Until we told him were going to be married,' Robbie
repeated. He threw up his hands and got to his feet, too
distressed to remain seated. 'Then all hell was let loose.
There was an almighty row. There was no talking to the
man. He did his nut!'

Lara moved on to the chair Robbie had vacated.
'Nikolai told me I must finish with Robbie straight
away, otherwise he would have no more to do with me,
ever! And then I told him there was a good chance I

was pregnant.' She looked down at the carpet, her lower lip caught between her teeth. 'I know it was a stupid thing to say. I—it was a—a desperate attempt to make him agreeable to the marriage. Of course it had just the opposite effect.' She looked apologetically at Janine. 'He was furious, crazy with anger. He turned on Robert and hit him—hard.'

'Look, that's the least of my worries,' Robbie began.

'But I never thought he would go that far!' Lara's eyes filled with tears. 'I'm well aware that my brother has a temper, but one rarely sees it—very rarely. I never dreamed he'd do something like that! Robert was knocked to the floor and——'

'That's how my wrist got sprained.'

Janine looked away from him, her heartbeat accelerating with anger. Fighting was simply not in Robbie's nature. She was appalled, envisaging the scene that had taken place.

But Robbie was philosophical about it. 'Don't look so cross, Jan. Actually, I can well understand his reaction. I mean, if someone had got *you* into trouble when you were eighteen—I mean, if I believed they had—and if he were years older—well, I think I'd have reacted the same way.'

Janine couldn't help smiling at that. Here was Robbie, seeing things from Nikolai's point of view. How typical of him! She took his point, though, even knowing he would have reacted with reason rather than violence. Her other brother, Peter, might well have reacted as Nikolai had reacted. Yes, Peter might well have reacted violently had Janine been in the same circumstances. Her anger dissipated. Nikolai Nekrassov was probably not as unreasonable as he sounded. 'Point taken,' she said.

'Of course I should never have mentioned pregnancy,' Lara said sheepishly. 'I told you it was my fault.'

'No, you shouldn't,' Janine agreed. 'It was stupid, as you say. I mean, you don't really suspect you're pregnant? Do you?' She tagged on the last two words, by no means certain Lara had invented it.

'No, of course not.'

'It wouldn't matter if you were, darling.' Robbie bent to give her a quick kiss.

Lara giggled. 'We've every intention of having children. But we have a few things to do before we start thinking about that!' The smile dropped from her face. 'And that's another thing!' she said heatedly. 'Nikolai might be rich, but I'm not—not yet. I have got some money, my inheritance from my father, and some shares in the business, but Nikolai is in control of it until I'm twenty-five. And he won't let me have a single franc of it! Nothing at all! And there's nothing I can do about that——'

Robbie dismissed that with a wave of his arm. 'Forget it, Lara. That doesn't matter in the least. I'm not exactly on the breadline! You mustn't care about——'

'I don't care about it. I don't care about money. It's—it's just *him*. He's being so bloody-minded!'

Robbie looked at his sister. 'It's true. His parting shot was, "Don't bother to go back to the restaurant— you're fired as of this minute!" Needless to say, we left when he started to get physically vicious. We stayed in a hotel for a few days because I couldn't drive very well with this.' He waved his bandaged wrist at her. 'And Lara hasn't got a driving licence yet. Besides, we wanted to be where nobody could find us, especially him. We drove back this morning. Lara and I had a great deal of talking to do, you can imagine. Our plans had to be adjusted somewhat.'

'And what exactly are your plans?' Janine settled back in her chair and listened to what they had to say. They talked to her for quite a while and as time passed she saw for herself how very deeply they felt for one another. She was very touched, pleased for them, and amazed at the realisation of what had happened to her brother in only three weeks. At length she said, 'Well, do you want my opinion? Now you've told me everything?'

'Of course.' It was a chorus.

'I think you should drive to Lille, right now, and talk again with Nikolai.'

'I agree,' said Robbie.

'No way!' Lara leapt to her feet, her arms waving about in agitation. 'You don't understand, Janine! You don't know what you're suggesting!'

'Yes, I do,' Janine said calmly. 'He's your only relative, Lara. You must talk again with your brother. You must try, at least. Otherwise your happiness will be marred by something as stupid as a family fight. I'll go with you if you like, to give moral support.'

'Oh, Jan, would you?' Robbie looked delighted at that but Lara was adamant.

'No. We're not going. Let him go to hell. I'm eighteen years old and I don't need anyone's consent to marry—not in France, anyhow. The age of majority is eighteen here. I don't need *him*! I don't need my money, his money, his consent or his friendship!'

'I was thinking only about the latter,' Janine said quietly. 'It would be so much nicer if you were friends, wouldn't it? If you—all of us—could talk him round? If he were there to see you married?'

When Lara was silent, Robbie answered for her. 'You're right, Jan. You're very wise. Lara is far more upset than she'll admit. For her sake, I'm prepared to talk to Nikolai again. As you say, he's her only relative and it's a sad state of affairs. Despite the tough front Lara is putting on, she'll be upset by this for a long time.'

Lara didn't deny it but she folded her arms stubbornly, sighing. 'Perhaps, perhaps. But I'm *not* going to Lille, and I don't want you to go, either. You're my life now, Robert. I can learn to forget that I ever had a brother. I will *not* go to Lille!'

Janine glanced helplessly at her brother. 'Lara, what did Nikolai's wife say about all this? Was she of the same opinion as he?'

The younger girl just laughed at that. 'Wife? Wife! Nikolai's not married! He'll never marry. He's thirty-five, and if he were capable of falling in love, he'd have done so by now. But he's not capable of it,' she added scathingly. 'He's too *hard* to feel emotions like——'

'That's ridiculous,' Robbie said patiently. 'He just hasn't met the right woman, that's all.'

'Oh, Robbie! Don't be naïve! He's met hundreds of women.' Lara turned to Janine. 'Don't misunderstand—I mean, there's nothing *wrong* with Nikolai,' she added, with a cheeky but humourless wink. 'He's not only met hundreds of women, he's also *had* hundreds. He's always got mistresses on the go! Right now he's got three of them. But love never enters into his relationships with women, he just—well, he works during the week, and during the week-ends he—he services his mistresses in Paris!'

Janine groaned inwardly. 'Lara, I really don't think——'

Her protest at these revelations was interrupted by Robbie. 'Now, Lara, calm down. Go and make us some more coffee.'

Lara did as she was told, without another word.

As soon as she had left the room, Janine and Robbie exchanged looks. 'You see what I mean?' he asked quietly, deliberately keeping his voice down. 'She's really distressed. She's not herself. You must disregard much of what she says about Nikolai—she's exaggerating wildly. Honestly, Jan. A week ago she was singing his praises to me! Right now she's just as angry as he is, that's all. The fact is, she loves him. The man's been like a father to her in many ways, being so much older. She respects him as she would her own father. She's terribly upset and she won't get over it in a hurry. Nothing will stop us from marrying, but—oh, I wish it didn't have to be like this!'

He paused, sighing as if all the troubles of the world were on his shoulders. 'I love her so much, and I don't want her to be upset like ... Would you go, Jan? Would you go and talk to Nikolai?'

'Me? You mean, alone?'

'*Please*, Jan. Would you? Maybe you can act as mediator.'

'Well ...' She was doubtful, unsure whether it was the right thing to do, to go alone. But her doubts were soon dispelled by the look on her brother's face. He looked both upset and—and hopeful that she would say yes. 'Okay, if you think it might work.'

'It might. It might. It's worth a try, eh? Oh, Jan, I'll be eternally grateful if you'll try!'

It was all settled by the time Lara came back. She took the news with incredulity, and Janine just laughed. 'Well, why not, Lara? He isn't likely to punch me, is he!'

She was joking, but Lara didn't seem sure. 'You can expect anything from him,' she said flatly. 'Nothing Nikolai does will surprise me. Nothing. Not after last Sunday.'

'Take my car, Jan. I'll write down the address for you.' Robbie left the room and Janine turned to Lara.

'It's Thursday. Is your brother likely to be at home when I get there?'

Lara shook her head helplessly. 'You're crazy—crazy but very sweet. I appreciate your motives, but you shouldn't go. It won't do any good at all.'

'Oh, he's had four days in which to get used to the idea. He'll have calmed down by now. Will he be at home?'

Again Lara shook her head. 'Nothing and no one will change his mind.' She shrugged helplessly. 'If he isn't at home, you'll find him at his factory.'

'His factory?'

'Sabre Cars. It's in Lille itself. Anyone will direct you.'

Janine's lips parted in surprise. *Sabre Cars?* 'Are you telling me that Nikolai——'

'He's the aerodynamicist on the design team.'

'Oh!' Janine laughed at what she'd been thinking. 'For a moment there I thought you were going to tell me he owns the place!' So Nikolai worked on the aerodynamics of those most prestigious vehicles. Sabre Cars were very big business indeed! Next to Rolls Royce they were heralded as the best cars one could buy—and were almost as expensive.

'He does own the place.' Lara's shrug was nonchalant then. 'He's a very rich and very clever man. He's also a dictator and a bully!' she finished angrily.

'Good grief . . .' No wonder the restaurant was little more than a hobby to the man! And his properties in Paris were probably nothing more than an investment of his spare cash. So this was why he lived in Lille, an industrial and manufacturing area . . .

Janine looked up suddenly, slightly put out by this new information. 'Lara, I think you should tell me something about your family, your parents and your brother. I—it might help me to understand him better, understand how his mind works.'

Lara did just that. She talked solidly for half an hour, and Janine was in no doubt that what she had heard was just the briefest description of the Frenchman—and the Russian family he was a descendant of. She felt better equipped now for her meeting with him.

She took the address Robbie had written down for her, took his car keys from him and slipped them into her handbag. Then a thought struck her. 'Hell's bells, Robbie! Mum and Dad!' With the onslaught of all she had heard during the past couple of hours, she had managed to forget why she had come to Paris in the first place!

'We'd better ring Mum now,' Robbie said practically.

'What are we going to tell her?'

'The truth, of course.' He cleared his throat, shifting uneasily where he stood. 'But we'd better play it down.'

'Quite.' Janine flinched inwardly as she looked at the swelling and bruising around his eye.

'Obviously we can't mention *that*. Or your sprained wrist.'

'Obviously.'

'Shall I speak to her first?'

'Yes. And like I say—play it down.'

They spent ten minutes discussing what they would say to their mother. They would stick to the truth—without alarming Rose—and make no mention of the one-sided fight.

Janine made the call. 'Mum? It's me. Well, there is a woman involved in this mystery. *Cherchez la femme*, I told you, didn't I?' She turned to look at Lara and her brother, keeping her voice light as she spoke to her mother. Provided there was no mention of the violence directed at Robbie, her mother would cope with what she was about to hear.

No, her parents would not be put out by what was happening. On the contrary, they would probably be pleased that Robbie had finally fallen in love with someone as nice as Lara. They had had him labelled as a perennial bachelor. And when it came to practical problems, Rose wasn't easily fazed. And of course there was nobody as down-to-earth as Archie. They would no doubt welcome Lara into the family as warmly and willingly as they had welcomed Peter's wife a couple of years ago. '. . . Your son has fallen in love and he's getting married. Yes, that's what I said! . . . But listen, there is a slight hitch. I'll let Robbie explain it to you. Hold on . . .'

Within the hour, having unpacked her case and changed her clothes, Janine was on her way to Lille. She spent the first fifteen minutes concentrating only on her driving, adjusting to being on the wrong side of the road again. After getting used to it she started giving some thought about what she would say to Nikolai Nekrassov.

She was not exactly looking forward to the encounter, nor was she put out by the prospect. She was by no means in awe of Lara's brother, in spite of all she had heard about him. He was only human, after all. Just a man.

Janine slowed down at one point, when she had left Paris far behind her, so she might enjoy the view. It was good to be in France again. She regarded it as her second home. Her mother's sister lived in Bordeaux, where Janine had spent many holidays as a child.

She put her foot down again. She must find somewhere to have a meal. Neither she nor the two lovebirds had given a thought to lunch, and she was ravenous. She giggled to herself, likening Robbie and Lara to Romeo and Juliet. But there would be no objection to this marriage from the Curtis family. Of course Lara was very young, but Janine for one was convinced that she knew exactly what she was doing. Still, time alone would tell, she realised.

She herself had had a proposal of marriage only six weeks ago, from a man she had known all her life, someone who had proposed to her twice before. Again she had said no, laughingly. She had no wish to hurt. She simply could not muster any enthusiasm over the man concerned, regardless of his wealth and the life he could offer. She would never marry for money—any more than Robbie would. What a nerve Nikolai Nekrassov had, implying that Robbie was a fortune-hunter!

As she pulled into the car park of a roadside restaurant, Janine checked that thought. She must, she really must, try to be neutral. Nikolai had his point of view. He was entitled to them. She must listen to whatever he had to say and try to remain unbiased in the matter. Robbie would want that. Robbie was a reasonable man, and she respected enormously that he had wanted to come personally to speak again with Lara's brother.

Her mission was very worthwhile. From what Lara had told her of the history of the Nekrassovs, they had been very much a family-orientated family. As the Curtises were. So what a pity it would be, how sad it would be if the two remaining members of that family, brother and sister, were doomed never again to speak to each other. It happened, of course—family feuds. But to Janine's way of thinking, it was unnecessary. To her way of thinking, there was nothing which couldn't be sorted out with a little give and take, a little reasoning.

Nikolai's house was difficult to find. It was several miles outside Lille, in the countryside, and the roads were poorly signposted. Three times she had to stop and ask directions, and the first two people were of no help at all.

It was dark now. She chided herself for having lingered such a long time over her meal. The darkness didn't help matters but she found the place, eventually. There was no other building in sight. Nikolai's house seemed to be in the middle of nowhere. If one didn't know, one wouldn't suspect that Lille itself, industrial and busy, was not very far away.

She steered her brother's small Citroën up a long and curving driveway, seeing that the gardens and surrounding grounds were untypically informal. In fact, from what she could see in the darkness, they looked fairly wild—yet not neglected.

The house looked immaculate from the outside. She saw it quite well by the light of an outside lamp and the streak of moonlight which brightened the sky as a dark cloud rolled away. The house, large enough to be called a château, was neither old nor new. It was built on two storeys and was very wide, but she could not see how far back it went. There was smoke coming from two of its chimneys and she could see lights through the shutters at all the downstairs windows except one.

She was glad, then, that it was late. She would much prefer to speak to Nikolai in the privacy of his home rather than at his factory. Nikolai. She was already thinking of him as if she knew him. Well, she did in a way. And whether he liked it or not, they were soon to become related, sort of.

A maid answered the door. She was dressed formally in black, her cap and apron white. Janine addressed her in French, her smile genuinely confident. 'Good evening, I would like to speak with Monsieur Nekrassov. Please tell him that I am the sister of Robert Curtis.' She repeated the English name to make certain the maid got it right.

'Oui, madame.' The maid, some ten years older than Janine, stepped politely aside.

'Mademoiselle,' Janine amended as she stepped into the hall.

'Pardon, mademoiselle. If you would please wait in the library, I will tell Monsieur that you are here.' She flicked on the lights as she showed Janine into a very impressive room.

Janine sat in a leather armchair, glancing around with interest. There was little to see other than the walls lined with rows and rows of books, but it was an impressive room, if a little austere. She could almost smell its atmosphere, or was that merely the cleaning spray which had been used on the vast, leather-topped desk and the leather furniture? Beyond the windows she could see nothing but darkness. Neither could she see the outline of another building. She wondered vaguely how many acres of land belonged to the house. It must be glorious, here, by daylight.

The maid reappeared, making a praiseworthy effort to hide her embarrassment but failing dismally. 'I— *mademoiselle*, I am sorry, but Monsieur Nekrassov is not receiving visitors this evening.'

At first Janine thought she had misheard. Of course, she had not. Furthermore, it was blatantly obvious that the maid was not conveying Nikolai's message verbatim. She wondered what the man had really said by way of a refusal to grant her an audience. Who did he think he was? Not receiving visitors, indeed!

'You told him I am Monsieur Curtis's sister?'

'*Oui, oui, naturellement* . . .'

Janine held up a hand, wondering how much the maid knew. Had she heard the row that had raged here four days ago? 'Very well, then please go and tell him again. My name is Janine—Janine Curtis. Tell him I have driven from Paris especially to talk to him.' Her composure was perfect, but behind it she was angry. She was slow to anger; she too had a temper which very rarely surfaced. But this was a little too much. Quietly, she went on. 'Tell him also that I have spoken with Mademoiselle Lara.'

The maid, who looked positively nervous, brightened at that. She left the room and reappeared in less than one minute. Nothing had changed. Go to hell, was the answer, though the maid didn't say that, of course.

Janine nodded, walked confidently out to the hall, then turned to face the maid. 'Which room is your employer in?' she demanded.

The maid pointed to a door, venturing no word of advice, no comment.

Janine walked confidently and assuredly to the door at the end of the hall. She did not bother to knock before she opened it.

CHAPTER TWO

THIS room was not as austere. It was given life, warmth, by the cardinal red of the carpet and velvet curtains of the same colour. The white walls were relieved by numerous paintings in elaborate frames. Again the furniture was leather, dark brown and deeply padded, comfortable-looking.

But that was all Janine had—an impression. She saw the room only from the periphery of her vision. Her eyes had travelled directly to those of the man sitting in a winged armchair by the fire, and having settled there she now seemed unable to look away. He was and he was not what she had expected.

On his lap there was an open book, in one hand a half-smoked cheroot, on a table by his chair an empty coffee cup. He was wearing a black velvet jacket and plain slacks, a crisp white shirt left open at the neck. He looked like a man who had settled down for a quiet evening after enjoying his dinner. A splendid dinner, no doubt. Oh yes, as far as all this was concerned Nikolai Nekrassov looked like what he was: a man of substance.

Janine held his gaze which turned immediately into a hard stare, speaking quietly and without hesitation. 'I have driven a hundred and fifty miles to speak to you, *monsieur*.' She left it at that, interested to see what his response would be, what she would gauge from it.

To her surprise he answered her in English, in a voice which was deep and cultured, totally without accent . . . but far from pleasant. 'Then speak, Miss Curtis, speak. And when you've said what you wish to say, get out of my house.'

He stood as he said the last few words, and Janine recognised the action for what it was: a deliberate psychological threat. It didn't work. She crossed the room and sat down in the fireside chair facing the one he had occupied, moving within three feet of him as she did so. He had succeeded in making her angry, but she did not feel threatened.

She was, however, extremely disconcerted. Not by his attitude—she had not expected this interview to be easy—but by the very sight of him. He was, she acknowledged detachedly, more than a merely handsome man. If any man could be described as beautiful, this one could. Seeing them together, no one would mistake Lara and Nikolai as anything other than brother and sister, regardless of the considerable age difference. He looked several years younger than thirty-five and the family resemblance was striking.

He was as positively masculine as Lara was feminine, but there was an intensity about Nikolai which she did not have. His hair was even darker than his sister's, as black as jet and naturally curly. It was crisp hair, healthy and plentiful but cropped close so that the curls were not allowed to have their own way. The effect was an intensification of the sculptured planes of his face. His bone structure was classic, the nose straight. His chin was square and the jawline strong and clean, but there was a hardness around the lines of his mouth. Beneath the blackness of his brows the eyes were incredibly blue—far deeper than the blue of his sister's and seemingly impenetrable, like the deep, dark blue of an ocean whose secrets had never been plumbed. They were intelligent eyes, cold as well as mysterious; cold, penetrating and watchful.

Janine slipped out of her jacket as she sat. She draped it over the back of the chair and looked into the flames of the fire, grateful for its warmth. A mild sense of shock darted through her as she discovered she was still seeing the face of her unwilling host. How strange. It was there, in the flames of the fire, as if every detail of it had been burned indelibly into her memory. She turned to look at him, her expression grave, wondering if this were some trick of the light.

One of his eyebrows rose slightly. 'So! The cook's sister is persistent if nothing else.'

It was an exquisitely executed insult. In a few words he had managed to put down both herself and her brother. The *cook's* sister . . . And he obviously believed she was *nothing* else. His tone of voice had made that abundantly clear.

Yes, he was, and he was not what she had expected. She had not been prepared to meet a man so incredibly physically attractive—but she had been prepared, from all she had heard from Lara, to meet someone hard, unsympathetic. He was more than that; he was conceited and arrogant in the extreme.

These thoughts went through her mind as she composed herself, crossing one slender leg over the other as she made herself comfortable. There had to be some way of getting through to him, and his attitude served only to make her more determined. She ignored his last remark. '*Monsieur*, let me say straight away that I understand your anxiety over Lara——'

'Get to the point,' he said tersely.

He was still standing. She watched as he flicked the half-smoked cheroot into the fire. He went to the drinks table and poured himself a cognac, obviously having no intention of offering Janine a drink. 'I'm waiting.'

She turned her hands palms upwards. 'I have got to the point. Your sister is eighteen years old and she has known my brother only three weeks or so. I want to say that I understand your misgivings about the marriage. Obviously.'

'Misgivings? Misgivings!' His voice was quiet and clipped, drenched in sarcasm. '*Mon Dieu*, the English propensity for understatement! I have *forbidden* Lara to marry your brother.' He turned to look at her. 'Now tell me, where is she hiding?'

Janine had no idea what he meant for a moment. Then she remembered that Robbie and Lara had stayed in a hotel for the past few nights. 'She isn't hiding, *monsieur*. She's in Robbie's apartment right now. Why, have you been trying to ring her? Does this mean you're prepared to talk about the marriage?'

He didn't even bother to answer that one. 'I have been informed that Lara has not been back to her rooms since she left here on Sunday. Nor has she attended the Sorbonne. Now, are you telling me she's moved in with Curtis, that they're *living* together?'

He was incensed by the thought. Fortunately his temper was harnessed at the moment, but Janine saw his eyes darkening.

She disabused him quickly. 'No, no, they're not living together. After leaving you on Sunday they stayed in a hotel some miles from here. They drove back to Paris this morning. They wanted to be certain of some privacy, you see. They wanted to make plans.'

He hadn't moved from the drinks table. He stood tall, straight-backed, an arrogant inclination to his head. Janine thought again of the family resemblance—and of the differences between him and his sister. Lara carried perhaps seven or eight pounds of excess weight, which was probably due to her youth. Because she was fairly petite she couldn't carry it off. But Nikolai Nekrassov was a good six feet tall and he had not an ounce of excess flesh on him. His face was lean and deeply tanned. Like his shoulders, his chest was broad, solid. Six feet of solid physique . . .

Dear Lord, Robbie was slight by comparison; he was certainly no match for this man when it came to . . . Janine let out her breath impatiently, her anger surfacing again as she thought of Robbie's black eye, the cut on his cheekbone. She was making a considerable effort to keep her bias in check, but she couldn't resist saying something about this incident. 'Besides, my brother wasn't fit to drive far with a damaged wrist and——'

'And a black eye.'

Janine sucked in her breath. If she had expected Nikolai to be contrite, she'd been wrong. He had spoken with satisfaction, as if he was proud of what he'd done to Robbie! Her heart sank. Would she get anywhere with this man? He had had four days in which to think things over and he was still behaving like the tyrant that he was. His anger had not dissipated, far from it.

'He can count himself lucky that I didn't kill him,' he went on, 'My sister told me she thought she was pregnant. Pregnant!'

'Well, she isn't,' Janine said firmly. Her clear green eyes held his. 'Think about it. They've known each other less than a month. I suppose you didn't stop to think——'

'It was not impossible.' He cut her off sharply. '*You* think about it! Besides, the fact that she could have been . . .'

Janine got the implication before he elaborated.

'. . . Curtis has seduced her. He's years older than she and he's mesmerised her into this sordid——'

'Don't be ridiculous!'

He spoke with a quietness that was chilling. 'Ridiculous, is it? Come now, Miss Curtis, you've seen them together. You're not about to tell me my sister has remained untouched?'

Janine looked away, disgusted. She thought of Robbie and Lara, young and very deeply in love. And here was this man, making it all sound so—so dirty.

In the face of her silence he went on. 'Exactly! And the girl is eighteen, innocent before he——' He didn't finish the sentence. There was a slight change in his attitude. He crossed the room and sat in the chair by the fire. Janine watched him cautiously, seeing the firelight reflecting on his dark features, his brown skin. What was he thinking now?

She cleared her throat. 'So you object to this marriage because of your sister's youth? *Monsieur*, don't you see that your behaviour last Sunday has only made Lara more determined? She admits it was stupid, saying that about being pregnant. You see, it was just a—a desperate attempt to get you to agree to the marriage. It was silly, but—well, that's how much she wants your agreement. Please don't turn your back on her. She doesn't want things to be like this——'

'The marriage will not take place. Lara is hardly more than a child. What does she know of life? She can think no further than a honeymoon! She doesn't know her own mind, so I have told her what to do.'

'As you always have.' Janine got nowhere with that remark.

'Yes, as I always have.' His eyes flashed in

annoyance. 'That is my role in her life. I'm her guardian. I'm here to protect her—from herself, if necessary. You spoke of my making her more determined. Let me tell you that I am aware of the tendency to rebel in those who are young. When I received Lara's letter telling me of this nameless and "marvellous" man she had met, I was amused. I realised that my little sister was starting to grow up. I acted wisely; I invited her to bring the man here so I could look him over. I was quite prepared to indulge her . . .'

He said it dismissively, with the wave of an arm, and Janine stared at him in astonishment at his conceit, his arrogance! How patronising could you get? He seemed to think that Lara had no mind of her own!

'. . . I would not have objected to her having an innocent friendship with someone I assumed to be a fellow student. Instead of this I find that my sister has become involved with one of my employees, a man who is a good deal older than she, and that he has seduced her and she is deluding herself into thinking she's in love——'

'She *is* in love.'

He looked at her contemptuously. 'Clearly you are an unrealistic romantic, Miss Curtis! Love? What is this thing they call romantic love?' he scoffed. 'What Lara is experiencing is an illusion! I don't profess to understand it, this thing that has taken over her senses, overruled her common sense!'

Janine made no attempt to enlighten him. If he were so ignorant of the emotion, he had obviously never experienced it for himself. So Lara was right about this much . . .

'It will run its course,' he went on, 'and die a natural death. Lara will discover for herself that this thing is unreal, ephemeral. In a week or so she will see how foolish she has been.' The hard lines of his mouth tightened in distaste. 'When she regains her senses she will regret as much as I what your brother has taken from her!'

There it was again, his anger at the thought of

Robbie and Lara being lovers. Or rather, his conviction that Lara had been taken advantage of. At least he realised there was nothing in the world he could do about that. He was simply waiting, now, for the affair to fizzle out. Quietly she said, '*Monsieur*, you're wrong if you think this relationship will be short-lived.'

He considered her before answering. 'Time will tell. Even so, she will not marry Curtis. I have given her my orders. She will not go against them.'

Janine was incredulous. He was absolutely convinced Lara would not go ahead with the marriage! Janine knew better. She also had a lot more to say to him. She had by no means given up yet.

But he leaned back in his chair, reaching for his box of cheroots as he dismissed her. 'You may go now, Miss Curtis. There's nothing further to be said.'

She smiled at him, making a very good job of hiding her annoyance at the way he was dismissing her. 'Would you be kind enough to pour me a cognac, *monsieur*? I have more to say to you, so I might as well be comfortable.' As she spoke, she got to her feet and moved the jacket from the back of her hair. She also took off the scarf she was wearing and then she sat down again, leaning back in the armchair just as he had done.

Silent seconds ticked by and she became nervously aware of her own heartbeat. She just didn't know what to expect. She had taken a chance. Would he throw her out bodily or would he do as she'd asked?

But she coolly maintained her composure while he insolently surveyed her from head to toe. Let him look, she thought, confident that her appearance, at least, could not be criticised. She was wearing a deep pink knitted dress which enhanced the curves of her body and suited her colouring. Janine's best attribute was her complexion, it was flawless and creamy, and she never wore skin make-up, only eye make-up and lipstick.

Nikolai Nekrassov surveyed it all, from the hair which fell loosely about her shoulders to the plain leather shoes she was wearing. He grunted. 'As a I said, you are nothing if not persistent.' He got up and poured her a cognac, refilling his own glass at the same time.

She watched him, biting back her retort. She was here for a specific reason and resorting to sarcasm would get her nowhere. It wouldn't help Lara. No matter what Nikolai was, in spite of the faults Lara had listed about him, he was still her brother and she loved him, respected him. The girl's tough veneer was transparent; she *cared* what Nikolai thought and his behaviour had upset her tremendously. And she would continue to be upset, as Robbie had said. Which in turn would affect Robbie.

Janine had to make Nikolai see sense. She had always regarded herself as something of a diplomat. Normally she got along with people—all sorts of people—with a natural ease that didn't even require thought. It was always she or her father who dealt with awkward clients in the travel agency, never their staff. It was she her friends turned to when they wanted advice or an opinion. She reasserted herself now, telling herself that her sensible and logical mind rarely let her down, that she would talk Nikolai round if she could just continue to be patient.

But there followed a totally illogical moment which surprised Janine so much that her well-rehearsed speech was momentarily forgotten. As Nikolai handed the cognac to her their fingers touched and it was as if she had suddenly become the conductor of electricity. It passed from him to her and sent a tingle along the skin of her hand, along her arm. It was not unpleasant, it was just . . . an alien sensation. She told herself quickly that she had either imagined it or it was in fact an electric shock; a freak, a fluke caused by some kind of friction.

But he had felt it, too. His eyes went immediately to hers and she saw his brows pull together in a frown, she saw the speculation in the deep blue of his eyes. Then it was gone, replaced instantly by the familiar coldness. He moved away from her abruptly. 'I'm waiting.'

The incident had thrown her and she looked at the carpet, trying to remember how she had intended to start her little speech. 'Robert wanted to come with me to see you. Like myself, he believes that this situation can be resolved to everyone's satisfaction if you would be prepared to talk—and to listen.'

'I don't believe that,' he cut in. 'Your brother hasn't the courage to face me again. He's sent you as his envoy.'

'Lara wouldn't come. Lara asked Robert not to come. You seem to have no idea how upset she is. She came here last Sunday to talk to you—they both did. But you were unreasonable, to put it mildly. She's not the child you seem to think her. She's mature, intelligent, and she knows precisely what she's doing. Please don't interrupt me again!'

To her surprise he let it pass, whatever it was that he had been about to say. Again she saw speculation in his eyes and again she deliberately looked away, finding this repeated surveillance off-putting.

'Robert and Lara had plans,' she went on, finally putting her thoughts in order. 'They intended to marry in Jersey, where Robert's family lives—as you're no doubt aware. Since you're Lara's only relative and Robert has several, they thought it sensible to marry on the island. They intended to honeymoon in warmer climes before returning to Paris where Robert would continue his work and Lara would continue her studies at the Sorbonne. She was prepared to do that, to complete her education, simply to please you. Actually, she never wanted to attend university in the first place. I'm sure you're aware of that, too. So you see, *monsieur*, your sister is not unreasonable. She knows the importance you attach to education and she would have done this for *you*.

'But they had to change their plans last Sunday. They can't marry in Jersey because Lara is under age according to the State rules. Being under twenty years old, she would need your permission as her guardian. However, they can marry in Paris, and that's what they're going to do. Lara refuses now to continue her studies. She and Robert are going to settle on Jersey after the wedding, provided she likes the island when she sees it. You see, there's nothing to stop her marrying in France, without your consent. The age of majority is eighteen here ... and there's nothing you nor anyone else can do to prevent them.'

'I don't intend to "do" anything,' he informed her. 'Because Lara will not go through with it. You don't know her, do you? You know hardly anything about her! Believe me, she will not defy me. I have brought her up to——'

'Nikolai, accept that it's going to happen. *Accept* it!' Janine used his name on purpose, speaking quietly but firmly. Surely, surely nobody could be as stubborn as he appeared to be? 'Listen to me, because this is what I really came to say, this is more important than anything else: there are two ways in which you can handle this situation. You can banish Lara from your life and never see her again, or you can be friends.

'I beg of you, let it be the latter. That way, you can continue to satisfy yourself that she's all right, that she's looked after—which she will be. If you shun her she could never turn to you if she does need help or support, if things do go wrong. Her pride would stop her from doing that. You see, I haven't come here to promise you they'll live happily ever after. Even they couldn't do that, as much as they might believe it. There are no such guarantees in life.

'There again, if things do work out well for them, then you'll have lost a sister, hurt her, and yourself, for what? You stand to lose so much that's precious in life, including the friendship of a caring family. My family— *Lara's* family. And you would never see her children when they do come along. So don't cut her out of your life, Nikolai. There's absolutely nothing to be gained by doing that. For heaven's sake, she's your only relative, you must at least wish her well!'

In the ensuing silence Janine became aware of rain beating against the windows. In the distance there was the rumble of thunder, but in spite of that and the rain, she could hear her wristwatch steadily ticking away. She didn't look at it; she didn't take her eyes from his.

It was a long time before he spoke. It was partly

because of this that she thought she had been successful in her mission. His silence pleased her, that and the way he was looking at her as if he were seeing her for the first time.

At length he stood and walked over to her. Standing directly in front of her, for the first time since meeting him she saw him smile. She saw the contrast of white and beautifully even teeth against the darkness of his skin, and then she looked into his eyes, expecting to find them quite different now.

They were quite different. They were filled with contempt, unmistakable contempt. For just a second this was added to by a glint of amusement. Then the amusement was gone. 'It was a pretty speech, Miss Curtis.' His voice was no more than a drawl. 'Pretty but hypothetical.'

Janine was stunned by what she'd seen in his eyes, incredulous at what he'd said. What a fool she had been in thinking she had got through to him! 'Hypothetical?' she said numbly. 'You're *still* convinced Lara won't go ahead with the marriage? Because you have forbidden it? She's an adult! You can't "forbid" it!'

Even as she spoke, she knew she was wasting her breath. There was no point in her staying here any longer. No point at all. She had said everything she could think of to get through to him. She had cajoled, she had been firm, she had tried appealing to his sense of duty, to his common sense, to his basic *brotherliness*! Nevertheless, she made one last effort before getting to her feet.

'Please, please will you talk to them? At least discuss it with them! They might be prepared to put the wedding off for a while if that would make you feel better about it. They're reasonable people, Nikolai. Believe me, they both realise their announcement came as a complete surprise to you.'

He was still looking down at her, shaking his head now as if he despaired of her, as if she were stupid. 'I told Lara last Sunday what would happen if she defies me. She will get *not one franc*——'

'She doesn't care about money. She cares about——'

'Me? Staying in my favour?'

'Yes. That's all she cares about.'

'Well, she won't have that, either. She will not see me or hear from me again, ever, if she goes through with this—this *mésalliance!*'

And there it was! *This* was the crux of the matter. Mésalliance, he had called it. He thought Lara would be marrying beneath her, marrying someone of a lower class—and that was his *real* objection! Janine had known it all along, of course. As Robbie and Lara did. It had been implicit in everything they had told her about Nikolai.

She stood abruptly, looking him straight in the eyes. 'So you've finally said it! This is what's really eating at you, isn't it? This is your main reason for objecting, "forbidding"? You think Robert isn't good enough to marry a Nekrassov!'

'I haven't made a secret of it, Miss Curtis,' he said coolly. 'If you were aware of it all along, why bother to give me all that sentimental rubbish?'

She had to get out of there, and fast. She absolutely would not allow this scene to develop into something nasty. It was bad enough as it was. If it turned into a verbal brawl it would only make matters even worse. She picked up her handbag and jacket. 'Because it's what I believe, it's what I think. I came here to tell you the marriage will go ahead, to tell you that your sister is genuinely in love with my brother. I came to ask you to be reasonable. But I did *not* come here to convince you of Robert's worth as a person. Lara is the only one who need be concerned about that.'

'And what is Curtis's worth?' he demanded. 'He's twenty-nine years old and he's achieved—what? The ability to cook well!' His laughter was scathing. 'I'd made my first million by the time I was twenty-five, and here you are telling me——'

'So that's how you measure a man's worth?' She spun on him furiously. 'By the size of his bank balance! I'm telling you this: when your sister marries my brother she'll be gaining far more than she loses—and I'm not talking about money! You spoke of your role in her life:

she's an adult, she doesn't need a guardian, she needs a brother. As her brother, all you can do now is to look on. That's your role now. And you should want to see her happy.'

'Happy?' he scorned. 'With a man like him? I can't even imagine what she sees in him! They have nothing whatever in common. *Who* is Robert Curtis? *What* is he? A sickly chef who can't even offer her a decent home to live in!'

He was wrong there. Robbie had a very nice home on Jersey—his own home, not his parents'. She did not put Nikolai right—on this or anything else. He had dismissed Lara's fiancé without any attempt to get to know him! She was appalled, disgusted at the way he had done this, at the way he had described Robbie as sickly. Sickly!

She flung her jacket on and made for the door.

'Wait a minute. Hear me out——'

'There is no point in listening to you!' She was shouting now. Her patience had run out and there was no hope of her being neutral. 'We don't speak the same language. We never did. You are pig-headed, arrogant and a snob—and what Lara sees in Robbie is something you will never understand!' She stalked out of the room, slamming the door behind her without giving him a backward glance. She strode angrily along the passageway leading to the vast hall, trembling inwardly.

The wind blew her hair over her eyes the instant she opened the front door and she was soaked before getting as far as the bottom step. The rain was coming down in sheets. It was bitterly cold and the wind was fierce, so strong that the rain was pelting horizontally.

'Oh, God, no! *No!*' Horrified, she stood transfixed, the lower half of her dress soaking up the rain like a sponge. She had left the car lights on and she was frantically praying that the battery wouldn't be flat.

She made a dash for the driver's seat, closing the door quickly against the foul weather as she hunted in her bag for the ignition key. The engine kicked into action at once, and she let out a sigh of relief. The thought that she might have to ask Nikolai Nekrassov for help had almost sickened her.

But the engine died before she even got into gear. She tried it again, and again it started ... and died. On the third attempt nothing happened. Nothing at all.

Janine didn't move. She switched off the dipped headlights and sat, thinking she would wait a few minutes and try again. Perhaps the rain had affected something or other in the electrics? If that were the case, she was doomed. Doomed to swallowing her pride and going back in that house to ask Nikolai Nekrassov for help. She looked at her watch. It was almost eleven and she had a three-hour drive ahead of her. At least the thunder hadn't moved any closer.

She waited ten minutes before turning the ignition key. The engine spluttered once before cutting out. It was hopeless. She glanced towards the door of the château. What chance was there of a garage being open in these parts at eleven in the evening?

She swore under her breath and it helped a little. She had, and she accepted the fact, no alternative but to face the man again. The door of the house wasn't locked and she let herself in, dripping on to the polished floor as she walked down the hall.

He didn't seem surprised to see her; he was just angry about it. 'Don't you ever knock?' he demanded.

Janine stood erect, her head high. 'Is there a garage around here, *monsieur*?'

The deep blue eyes raked over her, but she was past caring what she looked like. 'There are two. They're equidistant.' His eyes went back to the book on his lap. He was dismissing her, just as he had dismissed their entire conversation, and had started reading again, as he had been when she had first walked in on him.

It was then, right then, that she started to hate him. Her fingers curled into fists, the palms of her hands itching to slap that beautiful and arrogant face of his. 'Then may I use your telephone? I need help with the car. It won't start.'

'So I gathered.' This time, he didn't even look up. 'Both garages are closed. You're in the country, or hadn't you noticed?'

Janine was short of breath. Her heart was hammering so fast in anger that she couldn't supply it with the oxygen it needed. 'Then would you kindly lend me your car for five minutes so I can put the jump-leads on it and give myself a start? The battery's flat.'

His air of boredom didn't fool her for a second. He was just as angry as she was. Luckily he was just as controlled. 'Jump-leads, eh? And would you know what to do with them? Have you got any?'

She met his eyes. They were smouldering. 'I—I suppose so. There'll be some in the boot, won't there? Aren't they supplied with the car? I—Robbie's car is almost new.'

'So how come the battery's flat?'

'Damn you!' she blurted. 'It's flat because I left the bloody lights on! Satisfied?'

When she saw the corners of his mouth twitch, it pushed her over the edge. 'You won't think that's funny if you have to put me up for the night, will you? No, dammit, I'm not certain there are jump-leads in the boot, but I'm sure you must have some. And yes, I'm capable of using them if you'll lend them to me.'

He moved rapidly. She saw him getting closer through the haze which was her fury and when his fingers closed over her wrist it was all she could do not to kick at him. But so much had happened in so short a time that it made her dizzy. She felt that shocking, tingling sensation again at his touch, then it was obliterated by the pain of his grip. All this, while at the same time she realised she might well end up sleeping in the car if she didn't calm down.

He had yanked her towards him so that her eyes were level with his throat. 'Don't,' he said quietly, 'don't ever speak to me like that again. You're the one who's in need of a favour, Miss Curtis. Kindly bear that in mind.'

'I'm sorry.' She couldn't, wouldn't, look at him. His nearness was making her feel hot. Or was it merely her own anger which was doing that? She kept her eyes on the growth of dark hair where his shirt was open at the neck. Anything—anything rather than looking into those steely eyes of his.

'So you're asking me to help you. Right?'

Janine got control of herself now. She was no longer in danger of striking out at him, she wasn't going to cut off her nose to spite her face. 'Yes.'

He let go of her, moving away from her with a look of disgust on his face. 'You want me to bring my car from its garage at the back of this house, in the pouring rain, park it next to yours so you can take pot luck with a pair of jump-leads you may or may not have?' He shoved his hands into his pockets, nodding towards the door. 'After you, Miss Curtis. I'll tell you what's wrong with your brother's car, and that's all. The rest is up to you.'

She wasn't sure what that meant, but she didn't stop to ask him. He was right behind her as she headed for the car.

'Give me the keys,' he said as they reached the front door.

'They're in the ignition.'

'Then wait here,' he flung over his shoulder.

Janine stood in the shelter of the doorway, watching him. He got behind the wheel and turned the ignition key once. Then he got out, closed the door, locked it and made a dash for the house. His velvet jacket was wet—probably ruined—and he shook his head, incredulous. 'I've had as much of you as I can take in one night.' He almost spat the words at her. 'You're out of petrol! There's nothing wrong with your battery!' He switched suddenly to French, muttering something about stupid women drivers.

She answered him in French. 'I'm not out of petrol. I filled the tank to capacity when I was halfway here!'

He looked at her as if she were lying. 'Are you sure that was today?'

'Of course I'm sure it was today! I've never driven the car before! I tell you there's plenty of petrol in there!'

'And was the gauge working, when you filled it? Did you happen to notice?'

'Yes. I didn't happen to notice—I *checked*.'

'Then you've sprung a leak.' He walked away, heading for the drawing room.

Janine followed him. 'A leak? But—but the car's almost new, I told you. And surely I'd have noticed.' She was speaking in English again. 'You must be mistaken.'

He turned, his frustration with her all too evident. As if exercising enormous patience, he said, 'Miss Curtis, I manufacture cars. What I don't know about cars isn't worth knowing. I've given you my diagnosis. You are stranded. You'll need a new petrol tank.'

'Stranded?' She couldn't believe it. Here? With him?

'Stranded.' He almost smiled then. 'For the whole of tomorrow, probably. You can't fix a leaking petrol tank with a sticking plaster—even you must know that.'

He was pouring himself a drink and he offered her one. She shook her head. What she wanted was a cup of tea. And something to eat, come to think of it. It was ages since she'd eaten. Dear Lord, to have to impose on this man's hospitality really went against the grain. But what else could she do? She was miles from Lille and if she spent the night in the car, she'd probably die from exposure.

Nikolai was looking at her expectantly now, waiting for her actually to ask the question.

She asked. There was no point in staying in this room any longer than was necessary. 'So will you put me up for the night? I'll ring the garage first thing in the morning.'

'Why, yes, Miss Curtis,' he said graciously, 'I will put up with you for the night. I will tell Céleste to prepare a room for you.' He flung his wet jacket on to the sofa and walked out.

Janine flinched at his sarcasm. There was nothing wrong with his command of English—put up with her, indeed!

She stood by the fire, shivering. She would have to ring Robbie. He and Lara were expecting her back tonight. She would have to let them know what had happened. She glanced at her watch and then looked around for a phone. She couldn't see one.

'I'll have to ring my brother.' She greeted Nikolai with this as soon as he came back. 'He'll be worried if he doesn't hear from me.'

'There's a phone in the library,' he said shortly. He didn't look at her and she didn't look at him.

'Thank you,' she said grudgingly. 'For everything.'

'You'll find the maid in the kitchen—the door at the back of the house. She'll show you to your room after you've made your call. In other words, don't disturb me again. Goodnight, Miss Curtis.'

Janine walked out without saying another word. What an arrogant, insensitive, inhospitable *pig*! If Lara *could* forget that he existed, she'd be doing herself a favour.

Janine was not pleased with herself. She always likened herself to her father in temperament, but she wasn't half as controlled. He would have handled this situation so much better; he was far more tolerant than she. Oh, she was cool most of the time, but there were occasions, like tonight, when her volatility broke through. She had inherited this from her French grandmother, and her temper, but they were traits which were latent in her most of the time. At least she had managed to keep her temper in check, more or less, and given the raw animosity shown by Nikolai Nekrassov that was something to commend herself for.

But she had failed in her mission. She had failed miserably after being so confident of getting through to Nikolai. These were the first words she said to Robbie, and she was answered with a short silence.

'Well, thanks for trying, Jan,' he said at length. 'So nothing has changed? Nothing at all?'

'Nothing at all,' she said dully. 'The laws he laid down last Sunday still stand. Lara will never see him again if she marries you, etcetera.' She laughed humourlessly. 'But he is totally convinced that Lara will not—dare not—go through with it. The man is something else, Robbie. He thinks he's living in Queen Victoria's day!' In the background she could hear Lara saying, 'I told you! I *told* you!'

'He won't even talk it over with you,' Janine went on.

'There's nothing you could say or suggest which would make him happy about this marriage. The top and bottom of it is that you're just not good enough to marry a Nekrassov.'

'Tell me something new,' Robbie muttered. 'So what time will you be back? Where are you now?'

Janine sighed inwardly, explaining about the car and Nikolai's diagnosis. 'I'm obliged to stay the night. It's raining cats and dogs here and I'm miles from town.'

Robbie was horrified. 'Oh, Jan, I'm so sorry. I mean—how embarrassing for you!'

'I'm not embarrassed,' she said quickly, truthfully. 'Why the hell should I be embarrassed? I'll join you tomorrow. Expect me when you see me.'

She put the phone down and went to look for the maid. Céleste was waiting in the kitchen. She had obviously finished work for the night, because she was minus her cap and apron.

'Céleste? Thank you for waiting. Would you show me to my room now?'

'*Oui, mademoiselle.* If you'll follow me . . .' The maid was looking uncomfortable again and Janine began to think she must always be like that. Maybe she was simply shy?

She followed Céleste up the stairs which led from the kitchen, thinking they were taking a short cut to the first floor. The kitchen was at the back of the house, quite a walk from the main staircase in the hall.

But the reason for the maid's embarrassment was soon made clear. As they reached the top of the narrow staircase, Janine saw a man in an old towelling robe. He nodded briefly then vanished into a room on the left. And he, too, looked embarrassed.

'That was my husband, René,' the maid explained. 'He looks after the horses and helps with the grounds.'

Janine said nothing. Things started falling into place as Céleste opened the door of the room next to the one in which she and her husand slept.

'I—Monsieur Nekrassov told me to put you in here.' Céleste hardly knew where to look.

Janine quite literally saw red. The room was

adequate, of course, but that was quite beside the point. There must be half a dozen guest rooms in this house—and here she was in the servants' quarters! Half a dozen *empty* guest rooms, and Nikolai had specifically, *deliberately* ordered that Janine be put in the servants' quarters!

CHAPTER THREE

SHE held on by a very thin thread. Gossamer-thin. Somehow, *somehow* she managed to stop herself from flying downstairs and delivering the slap across the face she had been itching to give Nikolai for the past hour. He had begun their encounter with an insult, and now—now this!

Céleste looked at her apologetically, motioning towards the bed. 'I—er—I will make up the bed for you, *mademoiselle*, if you say so.'

'Don't bother.' Janine's voice sounded strange to her own ears. 'I take it Monsieur Nekrassov told you not to make the bed.' It wasn't really a question. Nikolai had obviously told the maid to leave linen on the bed, folded, so that Janine would have to make it herself. He certainly liked to add insult to insult!

'I'll do it for you——'

'No.' Janine put her hand on the maid's arm. 'I shan't be sleeping in here, so don't bother. Are the beds in the guest rooms made up?'

'*Oui* . . .'

'Then I shall make myself comfortable in one of those rooms. Don't look so worried, Céleste. This has nothing to do with you. I shall speak to your employer about it.'

'I—have to go down to brew coffee for him. Shall I bring you a cup?'

'Bring me a pot of tea, would you? And what is there to eat? I'm very hungry.'

'Sandwiches, *mademoiselle*? Or I could make——'

'Sandwiches will be fine. Anything will do.' Janine hooked her jacket over her shoulder. 'Come with me.'

She settled for the second room Céleste showed her in the main part of the house—a large room with an en-suite bathroom. When she was equipped with fresh towels and some soap, she dismissed the maid and ran a bath. She stripped to her pants and bra and hung her damp dress in the wardrobe. Then she wrapped herself in a bath towel and searched in her handbag for something with which she could tie up her hair. But her hands were trembling so much that her fingers seemed useless. She was absolutely seething, and the fact that she had counteracted Nikolai's attempted put-down was of no comfort. In the morning, she would give him a piece of her mind! In the morning she would say all the things she had refrained from saying tonight.

She didn't have a hairbrush with her, just a comb and a ponytail clip. That would do. She combed her hair up and clipped it in place, looking at her eyes in the mirror. They were very green, very clear and unnaturally bright, sparkling with the anger churning inside her. And her creamy skin was flushed and pink.

Who the hell did he think he was?

Nikolai Andreivitch Nekrassov, that's who he was. *Count* Nikolai Andreivitch Nekrassov, in actual fact. Oh yes, this family had quite a history! Janine had had a summary of it from Lara, and it had made fascinating listening. But Nikolai, the Frenchman with the Russian name, did not use his title. That was something. At least in that respect he was sufficiently into twentieth century France to realise that third generation Russian Counts were not revered as they once used to be in the old country. Yet he still demanded the——

The comb dropped from her hand as her bedroom door opened, as her bedroom door was *kicked* open. It swung back on its hinges and slammed against the wall. It all happened so quickly. She saw his reflection through the dressing table mirror and she spun round to face him, her lips parted in astonishment.

He was holding a tray on which there was a teapot, a cup and saucer, a plate of sandwiches and a side salad.

Janine was dumbfounded—by his dramatic entrance, by the sight of him holding a tray but mainly by the expression on his face.

He was leaning casually against the door-jamb now, watching her, laughing at her. It was genuine laughter, too. His eyes were lit up by it and Janine could do no more than stare at him as he walked towards her.

He lowered the tray on to the dressing table in front of her, letting it drop at the last moment so that everything on it rattled. 'Your tea, madam. And your supper.' His voice was a mixture of sarcasm and amusement. 'I trust madam now has everything she wants?'

Janine shot to her feet. She was barely two feet away from him. 'So you thought that was funny, did you? That was your idea of a joke, putting me in the servants' quarters?'

'No,' he said simply. 'What amuses me is your audacity in changing rooms without consulting me. That and the orders you gave to my maid.' He nodded towards the tray. 'A presumptuous sort of girl, aren't you? As well as persistent.'

Only then did she remember she was wearing nothing but a bath towel over her undies. 'How dare you walk in on me! Get out of here!'

His eyes moved insolently over the bare skin of her shoulders. 'I never heard you knock before you walked in on me. You did it twice, if I remember correctly . . .'

'Get *out*!' Janine was so angry she could hardly breathe. He was standing with his arms folded, his eyes coming to rest on the swell of her breasts which were only half covered.

That was enough. It was more than enough. The gossamer thread snapped and she slapped him without even thinking about what she was doing. With the open palm of her right hand she slapped him for all she was worth.

But she had no time to enjoy satisfaction in what she had done. Within split seconds of delivering the blow, he slapped her back. He slapped her so hard that it sent her backwards and sideways.

She half-screamed in fear and disbelief, her arm coming out to steady her against the dressing table. Then his hands were suddenly around her wrists and her arms were pushed behind her, and before anything was comprehensible to her, she found herself with her back against the wall.

With one hand Nikolai held both her wrists in the curve of her spine, his other hand clamped against her shoulder as he held the upper part of her body flat against the wall. Janine raised her knee, swiftly, aiming for that place where it would hurt him most. She wasn't quick enough. He moved so fast that she realised he had anticipated her action, stepping backwards with such speed that her knee moved against thin air. But he didn't release his hold on her as he moved and as a consequence she lost balance and fell against him.

'You bitch!' He shoved her against the wall again. 'If you try that again you'll find yourself on the receiving end!'

Janine gasped, terrified, in no doubt that he meant what he said. To her horror she realised that the towel had dropped from her body in the scuffle. Nikolai's eyes had darkened in anger, darkened so they were almost navy blue. They moved over her indolently, his hands tightening their hold on her as if to remind her she was helpless.

She started screaming, her eyes shut tight against the unbearable humiliation of what he was doing to her, the way he was looking at her body. The scream was cut off in mid-air as he covered her mouth with his own and he closed the space between them so she could feel the entire length of him against her. She wrenched her head away, nauseated by what he'd done. 'Get away from me, you animal! *Animal*!'

He laughed at her, but there was no humour in it this time. He let go of her shoulder, took hold of her chin and wrenched her head so that she was looking up at him. 'You've pushed me too far. You've taken too many liberties, *Miss Curtis*. Just like your brother! And how would he feel if he could see you now? How would he *feel* at the thought of someone taking *his* young sister? Someone who was years older and more than——'

'You're crazy!' Janine couldn't believe her ears, couldn't believe he was drawing a comparison between ... Then the implication of his words hit her and the breath rushed from her lungs in a cry of horror. She was petrified. Petrified by his intention, by the ice-cold intensity in his eyes, by the sheer physical size of him. If he meant what he said, she would have no chance against him. No chance!

Tears sprang to her eyes, tears of fear and frustration because the only way she could fight him was with words. And even those seemed to have deserted her, she was so appalled. He had lost his mind, she was convinced of it. His fury with her was so immense that he wasn't thinking straight. He wasn't thinking at all. 'P-please,' she stammered. 'Nikolai, please—I—there's ... there is a difference, you know.' He was still holding her chin so that she had to force the words out. 'You—you're not talking about lovemaking, you're talking about rape. Rape!'

Her eyes closed involuntarily and the tears spilled over, trickling slowly down her cheeks and on to the tips of his fingers. They came open again instantly as the grip on her wrists was released. At the same time, he took his hand from her face, his thumb brushing over the tips of his fingers as if her tears had scalded his skin.

Janine was free, but she didn't move a muscle; he was still standing very close to her. Her heart was hammering against her ribs and she watched him very, very cautiously, by no means convinced of her safety.

Through the thin material of his shirt she saw his chest expand as he took a deep breath and let it out very slowly, his eyes closing briefly as he did so. Then he was looking at her. 'Stop that,' he said quietly, almost softly.

He was controlled. She was safe. Her heart slowed down a little, but she couldn't just switch off the tears. They kept coming, noiselessly. She swallowed and it sounded loud in her ears. Then there was silence, absolute silence in the room, the house.

Still she watched him, unmoving. She was leaning against the wall and he was standing at arm's length, running his fingers through the crisp, short curls of his hair. The silence was like a third presence in the room and it was seconds before he spoke. 'Rape?' It was as if he were speaking to himself. 'No.' He shook his head slowly, his voice barely audible. 'Oh, no, never that.'

Janine's heartbeat slowed to normal and her vision cleared as her tears stopped coming. She couldn't take her eyes off him. She was no longer afraid but fascinated. In spite of everything, she wanted to know what was going through his mind now. She wanted very much to know that.

His eyes moved to meet her gaze and she saw in them something . . . something approaching . . . She thought it was sadness but knew she must be mistaken. For the first time she saw his eyes for what they were—very beautiful. Beautiful and expressive, a mirror to his thoughts now, though she could hardly believe what she was seeing.

Again there was silence, an unnatural stillness as they stood, looking deeply into one another's eyes. Questions were being asked by both of them while not a word was spoken. Who are you? What are you? What are you thinking now? What are you feeling?

Without realising what she was doing, as though she were watching herself in a dream, Janine found herself stepping towards him at the precise moment that he reached for her. He put both hands on her shoulders, lightly, gently, as his lips came down to brush against hers. Janine's head moved back slightly, her lungs filling with air as the touch of his hands, his lips, made her gasp. Waves of shock rippled through her body, leaving her trembling and weak. Her skin tingled not only where he touched her but where he might touch her . . .

Still his lips were caressing hers only lightly. Touching and separating, touching and separating. Her lips were parted, tasting, exploring, experimenting. This discovery was something to be savoured, tasted slowly. It was too powerful, too intoxicating to drink of quickly.

The kiss began properly as Nikolai's fingertips moved along the contours of her shoulders to the delicate skin of her neck. His fingers slid into her hair as he moved her head gently closer and he kissed her more deeply. It was, for Janine, as if she were functioning on two different levels. It was dreamlike as if her mind, her common sense, stood apart from all this. Apart and looking on. She could hear what it was trying to tell her—that she was the one who had lost her senses now; that she would regret these moments till the day she died; that Nikolai Nekrassov was despicable and the epitome of everything she disliked in a man.

Nevertheless she saw herself responding to him. She saw his fingers tightening in her hair as he continued to kiss her. Then her hair had loosened from its clip and was falling around his hands. But her mind, that part of her which was watching and protesting, switched off suddenly and she knew only the darkness of her closed eyelids.

The Frenchman's kiss held her captivated. Her mouth opened beneath his and tasted fully the warm firmness of his lips. Physically she was powerless to stop him. The more he kissed her, the more she wanted, and as he explored the moist warmth of her mouth, she responded with passionate encouragement.

His breathing coarsened as his hands moved downwards over the bare skin of her back. His fingers closed on the slenderness of her waist as he pulled her body tightly against his own. It was only then that sanity returned, that her mind and her body were one again. They were one and they were at war. For mere seconds her body persisted in pressing against the hardness of him, then her mind at last took control and she stepped away from him abruptly.

Her breasts rose and fell as she struggled to breathe normally again. Nikolai was staring at her, his disbelief, his bewilderment, equal to her own. She did not want him to see her confusion, did not want him to read the questions she was asking now. Yet she couldn't look away. What *was* this? What was this—this appetite which had grown with feeding? How could it happen?

How could such a tremendous force develop so quickly—so quickly and between two people who had not the slightest thing in common, who actively disliked each other?

He was thinking, feeling, exactly the same things. She knew it. He knew she knew it. In those minutes there had been, there still was, communication between them in the form of questions. Yet not a word had been spoken. Not a single word. It was only their breathing which broke the silence. Janine was trembling from head to foot, almost hypnotised by what had happened.

The spell was broken, shattered, as she stepped further away from him. He was reaching for her and she dared not allow him to touch her again. 'Get out, Nikolai.' She said it softly, turning her back on him as she spoke. She was no longer afraid of his anger. She was not afraid of him. She was afraid of the discovery she had made. She was afraid of herself.

She was also filled with self-loathing, just as she had known she would be during those seconds when her mind and her body had divorced. How she could willingly have succumbed . . . encouraged . . . *instigated* what had happened . . . No, no, they had joined together simultaneously, thinking and feeling as one. And she would never understand it. For as long as she lived she would never understand the insanity of the past five minutes.

The door closed quietly as Nikolai left the room, and Janine's body sagged with relief. Inwardly she was near hysteria. She sank to the floor, leaning against the dressing table stool as she reached for the bath towel.

The rain had stopped. It must have stopped some time ago. Irrationally she thought of dressing and just—just walking away from the château. But there was nothing to worry about now. Nikolai would not come into her room again.

She sat there, bemused, thinking a hundred thoughts which got her nowhere in trying to understand what had happened. At length she took hold of herself mentally. She was making too much of it, surely? Surely it was a simple case of sexual—purely physical—

attraction. And so what? Granted, she had never known this before, nothing of this magnitude at any rate. But what of it? *Why* did she feel afraid of it?

She would never see Nikolai Nekrassov again. Not after tomorrow morning. There were at least two things which she could be sure of: Lara would marry Robbie, and Nikolai would carry out his threats. She could be confident of both those things ... which meant she would never need to face Nikolai again, after tomorrow.

Janine got to her feet and looked at her reflection in the mirror. She was as good as naked in a low-cut bra and bikini pants. There was nothing about her figure that could be criticised. She was slim yet curvaceous, openly admired by the opposite sex. Maybe this and her lack of clothing had caused Nikolai to get heated? But they had begun by fighting, for heaven's sake! Literally, physically, fighting!

The word hate was a strong one, one that Janine used as infrequently as she used the word love. These words described powerful emotions; they should not be used lightly, insincerely. But she had hated Nikolai Nekrassov within an hour of meeting him and she was not going to amend that now, no matter what had happened between them. She hated him; there was no other word for it.

As her eyes moved upwards towards the reflection of her face, she blinked in surprise. She looked wild. Her face was flushed, her eyes were as bright as they had been when she was furious and her hair was tumbling all over the place.

Again she looked at the length of her body. She could still feel the touch of his hands, still feel the warm hardness of him as he had held her against him. The vividness when recalling how his lips had moved against hers was shocking to her. She felt branded, branded and soiled.

The bath had cooled off, so she topped it up with hot water and got into it, under it, washing her body and her hair as if she could swill away the invisible marks he had left on her. It didn't work. Worse was the discovery that when she closed her eyes against the memory of him, she could still see his face, every handsome detail of it, as clearly as if he were standing before her. As clearly as she had seen it in the flame of the fire, mere seconds after meeting him.

Janine hardly slept that night. It was a long, long time before she drifted into something which was barely more than a doze. Even then she snapped into consciousness several times, wondering where she was and then remembering . . .

It had been quite a day. Since leaving Jersey in the morning she had learnt and experienced so much that it was hardly surprising she couldn't sleep properly. But she did sleep well eventually. When daylight stole through the beige, silky curtains, she fell into a deep and dreamless sleep. Probably it was due to her physical exhaustion, or maybe it was simply that she felt safer when daylight came.

She pondered over that when she finally woke. She knew it must be late, but she had no idea of the time, her watch had stopped during the night. There was no movement, no sound coming from the house.

On the dressing table was the pot of tea she hadn't touched, the sandwich curled at the edges. She got out of bed and peeped through a chink in the curtains, conscious of her nakedness and not wanting to be seen. She blinked several times against the light, smiling at the magnificence of the view. What a perfectly lovely place to live! She could see for miles, miles of greenery, fields and woods. The sky was clear and a pale sun was shining. There were a few buildings around after all; she could see a farmhouse with outbuildings, another residence off to the east, and in the distance the gentle curve of a river.

Living on an island made one appreciate vast open spaces such as this. There were occasions when she felt a little claustrophobic, living on Jersey. But the feeling passed. It was her home, after all, and she liked it very much. Janine knew Jersey like the back of her hand. Perhaps that was a disadvantage; there was nothing left for her to discover. Was that why she had been unable to settle properly during the year she had been back? She turned from the window and headed for the bathroom, thinking about home and the man who wanted to marry her.

She—all the Curtis children—had known Michael Granger all their lives. He had been at her other brother's wedding and he would be at Robbie's. Michael and Robbie had gone to school together until Michael had been sent to a public school in England.

Janine was eighteen when he had first proposed to her, eighteen and by no means ready to settle. She thought of Lara then. Was Lara ready for marriage? Was she, actually? Could Nikolai possibly be right in saying Lara was thinking no further ahead than the honeymoon? No, Lara and Robbie had spoken of their plans for the future, albeit with several ifs and buts.

In any case, it was impossible to compare herself and Lara at the same age. Lara was madly in love, and that was something Janine had never experienced. But she didn't scoff at the concept as Nikolai did. She had never experienced it personally, but that didn't mean it was unreal, non-existent.

Michael Granger professed to be in love with Janine. If he was, she felt sorry for him. She respected the emotion sufficiently to realise that it must hurt like hell if it was unrequited. And Michael was something of a playboy and she doubted very much that he meant what he said. Oh, he liked her well enough, there was no doubt about that. But they were used to each other; they had known one another for so long. Janine liked him, too, but that was all. She could stretch things no further than that. She certainly didn't love him. Except, perhaps, in a sisterly way.

No. What was she thinking about? Of course Michael wasn't in love with her. Michael was rich and spoiled; he only wanted what he couldn't have. She went out with him these days only when she felt bored and had nothing better to do. He knew this. He knew it because she told him quite bluntly, much to his amusement. He fancied himself enough to think she was lying, to think it was just a female ploy—a game of playing hard to get.

Janine was hard to get. Michael Granger did not have a hope. If she had a pound for the number of times she had staved off his advances over the years, she could buy herself a mink coat.

The thought pulled her up short.

She was in the midst of brushing her teeth with her finger. (She found toothpaste in the bathroom cabinet, but she didn't have a toothbrush with her). She rinsed her mouth and dabbed at her face with a towel, looking at the bathroom floor as if she might see written there the answer to the questions in her mind.

Michael Granger was likeable and a good friend. He was attractive and sophisticated and he wanted to marry her. Yet she had never allowed him to go further than kissing her. Why?

Nikolai Nekrassov was a total stranger about whom she had been told a lot of unpleasant things. She had discovered for herself his abhorrent personality, his insensitivity, his overwhelming arrogance. Yet only a few hours ago she had wanted him in the fullest sense of the word.

Why?

Why had she wanted Nikolai Nekrassov when she had never even considered making love with Michael? What was it about the Frenchman that had attracted her so? Chemistry, they called it, those who attempted to explain such things.

She threw the towel into the linen basket. Chemistry. Something in the man which called out to the woman, and vice versa. How basic, she thought. How animalistic when there was nothing else between the people concerned!

That feeling of self-loathing was still very much with her. She dressed and made up, taking her time about it. With luck Nikolai would have gone off to his factory and she wouldn't see him. She would ring the garage and go with the man who came to tow away the Citroën. She would while away the hours until the car was fixed and then drive back to Paris and things that made sense.

All she wanted now was to forget that Nikolai

existed. As Lara would have to do. It would be easier for Janine, though. Much easier. Poor Lara . . .

Janine went into the kitchen first. Céleste was there, and an older woman who was taking freshly baked bread from the oven. The smell of it reminded Janine how hungry she was, and she looked up to see the cook smiling at her as if she had read her mind.

'*Bonjour, mademoiselle.*'

'*Bonjour*, Céleste. Has Monsieur Nekrassov gone to work? What time is it, actually?' Janine started winding her watch.

'No. He's waiting for you in the dining room. It's eleven o'clock, *mademoiselle*. Eleven, exactly.'

Janine thanked her and headed for the dining room. He had to be faced. She was both irked and disappointed to learn he was still in the house. It was Friday today; why hadn't he gone to work? She was also annoyed with herself for sleeping so late and for not asking Céleste to wake her early. She had to get the car repaired, and time was marching on.

Nikolai was standing by the window. He was just standing, looking out, seemingly miles away in his thoughts. He was wearing riding boots, tight black denims and a black rollneck sweater. He looked formidable, almost menacing as he turned to face her, unsmiling. 'Good morning. You slept well, I take it?'

'Eventually.' Janine looked away and sat down at the table. He had already eaten, but there was a place set for her. She had been composed before she walked in to this room. Now she was jumpy, nervous, and she hated herself for it because she didn't understand it. She gestured towards the table, unable to prevent her sarcasm. 'This surprises me. I should have thought you'd want me to take breakfast in the scullery. Wouldn't that be more fitting?'

He ignored the remark completely. 'Your brother's car has been towed away—I phoned the garage first thing. I'll give you a lift into Lille and you can wait for it. It should be ready at four o'clock.'

'Thank you.' She said it grudgingly, still avoiding his eyes.

'Why are you using your brother's car? Don't you have one of your own?'

'Yes, but I didn't bring it with me. I flew to Paris from Jersey.'

She sensed rather than saw his look of surprise. 'I—just assumed you lived in Paris. I didn't realise you lived in Jersey.'

'With my parents.' She glanced at him then. He was still standing by the window, and his back was towards her again.

'And what do you do with yourself there? How do you earn your living?'

His questions surprised her. He wasn't the type to make small talk. 'Tell me, why the sudden interest in Robert's family? Are you having second thoughts about the marriage?'

'I'm asking you what you do, that's all.' His voice was clipped. She had succeeded in annoying him and she was glad. She knew very well he wasn't having second thoughts.

'I don't do anything,' she said airily. The devil was in her this morning and she couldn't seem to do anything about it. 'I'm the Empress of the Channel Islands. Didn't you know that?'

He was not amused. He turned to face her, his eyes flashing dangerously, but she didn't give a damn.

Céleste came in before he had a chance to say anything. 'What can I get you, Mademoiselle Curtis? Cook asked me to tell you she has fresh croissants, piping hot.'

Janine didn't need tempting. Normally she didn't eat breakfast, but she was starving this morning, and when in France she never could resist hot croissants. She asked for three and a pot of tea.

'Well?' Nikolai demanded as soon as they were alone. 'It was a civil question, was it not?'

'Then I'll tell you,' Janine shrugged. 'I'm on holiday at the moment. I don't really live with my parents. I live in London and I'm a tap-dancer with the Royal Ballet Company.'

'Janine——'

It was the first time he had used her name; it registered with her. But he was wasting his·time in trying to be civil. Her hatred of him was almost trickling out of her pores, and she would never forgive the way he had tried to put her down last night with that business in the servants' quarters. Nor would she forget what had taken place later. She hated herself for that as much as she hated him for it. 'What difference does it make?' she snapped. 'You're not interested in me any more than you're interested in the man your sister's going to marry! I'm a scullerymaid at Ten, Downing Street. There, does that ring true? Will that shut you up?'

She instantly regretted her outburst. What was wrong with her? She didn't normally behave like this. Not ever. Not with anyone, no matter how much she might dislike a person.

There was an ominous, dangerous, silence.

Her stomach contracted nervously. There was that unnatural stillness again. She was asking for trouble; Nikolai's threshold of tolerance was very low indeed. 'I'm sorry.' She looked up him quickly, seeing the muscle working high in his jaw. The deep blue eyes were boring into her, not asking questions now, but warning her. She apologised again. 'I—it's just that I'd rather be alone while I have my breakfast. I'm—not one for making small talk first thing in the morning.'

'Neither am I,' he said quietly. 'At any time of the day.' He walked towards the door. 'I'll go and change. You'll find me in the drawing rooom when you're ready to go.'

Janine was embarrassed when they stepped out of the front door half an hour later. There on the gravel of the driveway was a huge dark patch, the last of the petrol which had leaked from Robbie's car. She apologised again because this really was a bit much. It looked awful.

Nikolai shrugged. 'Shall we say that you have certainly left your mark while visiting this house? Wait here, I'll bring my car round.'

She had levelled off a little emotionally. Her need to attack him had lessened enough so she could at least attempt civility. But she was almost counting the minutes until she could get away from him.

That thought went out of her mind, however, when she saw his car, and civility came easily to her. It was out of this world! Sabre cars were custom-built, sleek, luxurious, with a performance no other car could equal. The one she was looking at was white, freshly waxed and polished, gleaming in the morning sun. She simply couldn't resist remarking on it; indeed, it never occurred to her to try. 'This is something else!' As she got into the passenger seat, her enthusiasm was plain to see. 'It's beautiful!'

In the face of his silence, she went on. 'There are a lot of wealthy people on Jersey, but there are only two Sabre cars on the island. Did you know that? I suppose you export a lot of them? I mean, I know you don't exactly mass-produce them!'

'Yes, a number of them are bought by Arabs these days.'

'I believe you work on the aerodynamics yourself?'

'Among other things. That's just one of my functions.' He paused, seemingly unmoved by her show of interest. Then he surprised her completely. 'Would you like to drive it into Lille?'

'You can't be serious?' Janine was taken aback, to say the least. Michael Granger had flatly refused to let her drive his Rolls, and here was Nikolai—of all people—offering to let her drive a car worth thirty or forty thousand pounds! She had no intention of accepting the offer, she just wanted to be sure if he meant it. This—after he'd called her a stupid woman driver only last night?'

'Why not?' he shrugged. 'I thought it would be a new experience for you.'

She frowned, meeting his eyes. This was the first time she had seen them in full daylight and they looked different again. Different and undeniably beautiful, framed by lashes as black as jet. 'I—er—it would. But the answer's no. Thank you.'

'Then fasten your safety belt.' He said no more. He switched the engine on and pulled away slowly, driving at a moderate speed, and in silence, for the first few miles.

Janine watched him without letting him know she was doing so. She watched him because she was unable to stop herself. His driving interested her. It told her things about him. He made no attempt to show her what the car was capable of, no attempt to impress her. He drove steadily, assuredly, with that air of self-possession which was so much a part of his nature. Nikolai Nekrassov knew what he was and who he was. He had no need to try to impress. Consequently Janine was impressed. She begrudged the fact, but she could not deny it.

She found herself wondering how she would have got on with him had she met him in different circumstances, had there not been this bone of contention between them. Not well, she decided, because she would have discovered what he was like eventually.

It was he who broke the silence. 'You realise I couldn't help you personally with the car,' he said at length. 'My factory is not geared for work on Citroëns.'

'Yes, I—realise that.' Again he had surprised her. Would he have helped if he could?

'I'm flying to Germany on business this afternoon,' he went on. 'So all I can do is drop you at the garage and then it's a question of waiting.'

She looked at him then. 'Fine. That's fine.' He was wearing a business suit of conventional cut in conventional grey. After this morning's riding boots and last night's dinner jacket, she felt she was seeing yet a different side to him. His attitude was different again, too. He knew who and what he was . . . but Janine was becoming less and less certain.

Nothing else was said. They were approaching Lille and an atmosphere was growing between them. His nearness was getting to her. Uninvited memories were crowding her mind and her pulse began to quicken. She had the insane idea that she wanted to touch him—his hand—his shoulder, just to see if it had all been a fluke, unreal. Would it happen, if she touched him, if she accidentally brushed against him? Would the electricity be there?

At that very instant, Nikolai turned to look at her, taking his eyes from the road for several seconds. She was convinced he had read her thoughts and she blushed stupidly, like a schoolgirl on her first date. She looked quickly away, turning her head to the window at her side. Dear God, he *had* read her thoughts! Either that, or he'd been asking himself the same questions.

They passed his factory. It was there, on the right, set back from the road and surrounded by railings covered in steel mesh and topped with barbed wire for security purposes. Over the entrance was an arched sign in wrought iron which read, simply, Sabre Cars. Sabre Cars—Nikolai's empire. Founded by his father and made by Nikolai into what it was today.

He drew to a halt at a garage in the centre of Lille, not switching off the engine as he turned to face her, his expression impassive. 'The mechanic has the keys to the Citroën,' he said, in a voice which could not be more neutral. 'I'd put them in my trouser pocket last night, remember?'

'I—yes, I remember.' She would never forget last night, not one single detail of it. 'Well, goodbye. Thank you for the lift.' She was anxious to get away from him and he was making no attempt to come round and open the door for her. She opened the passenger door.

'Just a moment, Janine.'

She froze, her heartbeat accelerating. But she needn't have worried. He hadn't stopped her by putting a hand on her arm, just with his words. He took from his pocket the scarf she had been wearing the day before. She must have left it on the sofa when she dashed from the drawing room.

'Thank you.' She took it from him, being careful not to touch him, no longer having the courage to get the answer to her question. 'I—there's—is there anything I can say to Lara? Any message you want me to pass on?'

'Just tell her I'll be waiting to hear from her as soon as she's regained her senses.'

'I see,' she said stiffly. 'Of course it would have to end like this. 'Then you'd better resign yourself to your fate: you'll never see your sister again!'

'So be it,' he said harshly. 'Then I shall simply regard her as dead!'

Appalled, Janine got out of the car and walked away without so much as a backward glance. She walked briskly out of his sight and out of his life.

CHAPTER FOUR

JANINE had been home for almost two hours and her parents were still asking questions, questions and more questions. Rose was asking most of them, and while Janine understood it she had nevertheless grown irritated.

Her parents had had a long telephone conversation with Robbie and Lara on the day Janine spent in Lille, and in a week's time the engaged couple were coming home. They would stay here, in the house, to give Lara a chance to get to know her future in-laws and to give Robbie the opportunity of showing her Jersey—her future home, if she liked the island. If she felt that she could settle here, they planned to live in Robbie's cottage, just a few miles away in Trinity.

Robbie had bought the cottage six years ago, before he started working abroad. In the summer he made a fair amount of money by letting it to holidaymakers, something which Archie managed on his behalf. At the moment it was empty, being out of season.

'But the place will have to be redecorated and refurnished if they're going to make it their home,' Rose was saying. 'Will there be time to do that before the wedding?'

Archie laughed at that, the corners of his eyes crinkling as he looked at her fondly. 'Rose! Don't jump the gun. Lara hasn't seen the place yet, nor the island. And we don't even know when the wedding will take place. We can't be sure of anything till the youngsters get here and we all sit down and discuss things.'

Janine couldn't help smiling at them. Physically her father was an older version of Robbie—a little broader, perhaps. He was the same height and had the same light brown hair colour. It was thinning on top, but there was no grey in it. He was puffing on his pipe now, unruffled by all the news Janine had passed on and a perfect anchor for his wife's over-excitement. And Rose was excited by the prospect of her elder son's marriage, very much so. She was also anxious as to whether Lara would like her, and vice versa.

Janine thought there was nothing to worry about in that respect—either way. The only shadow on the entire business was that which Nikolai Nekassov had cast. That was the reason she had grown irritated: her parents had questioned her about Nikolai and she had been loath even to speak about him, keeping her opinion of him down to a few words—a few basic, uncompromising and accurate adjectives.

'Well, I'm off to bed,' she said then. 'Think I'll take a bath and have an early night, if you'll excuse me.'

'Hang on, love.' Her father waved her back into her chair. 'I'd like to hear more about this brother, Nikolai. I'm intrigued.'

'Intrigued?' Her tongue clicked in irritation. 'It's very straightforward, Dad. There's nothing to be intrigued about. I've explained the whole situation to you, there's nothing more I can add.'

There was a great deal more she could have added, but for obvious reasons she wouldn't. She had told her parents of the conversation, and the row, she had had with Nikolai on the evening she was obliged to stay in his house. She had told them of his parting shot the next day, when he drove her to the garage. But she had not said a word about the fraught scene which had taken place in her bedroom. Nor had she mentioned that Robbie was walking around with a black eye and a sprained wrist. She and her brother had agreed that he would explain that away when he got to Jersey.

For Rose's sake, Robbie would lie about how he got

the bruise. Their mother, they felt, had quite enough to cope with as it was. She was already distressed over the business of Nikolai—on Lara's behalf. She was anxious about meeting Lara, anxious about the age difference between her and Robbie—or rather, the fact that Lara was so young. This, while at the same time she was already planning the wedding and who she would invite!

'Yes, I want to hear more about him,' Rose said then. 'I can understand his thinking his sister is too young to marry. I can understand his being shocked—after all, she's only known Robbie a short time. We're all surprised. But I can't understand his saying he'll regard his sister as dead if she goes ahead with the wedding. It's awful—and pointless.'

'It's a question of pride,' Janine said patiently. Deliberately she added, 'I've told you what it's really about. He thinks Lara is marrying beneath her, the wrong type, the wrong class. Mum, just forget about him, as Lara will. He's conceited, a snob. He isn't worthy of discussion, and he's certainly not the sort of person you'd want to be involved with.'

'That's a strange thing to say.' Archie looked up suddenly, frowning. 'Isn't that kind of ... reverse snobbery? Jan, that's the very attitude you're resenting in him!'

'*I'm* resenting? Don't you resent it?'

'I'm reserving judgment,' Archie said simply. 'I'm keeping an open mind. I'll make up my mind when I meet him, and not before.'

Janine looked heavenward, impatient. 'Haven't you been listening to me? You'll never meet him, don't you understand that?'

Her father looked at her steadily, seeming vaguely disappointed. 'Yes, I was listening to you. You poured out a stream of abuse; it was nothing short of that. And that isn't like you, Jan, regardless of the things the man said about Robbie. Haven't I taught you always to look beyond the surface, to ask yourself *why* people behave the way they do?'

'Yes, you have. And I did. And I found the answer.

I've given you my opinion—my considered opinion. Have you lost faith in my judgment? Can't you take my word for it, Nikolai Nekrassov is as hard as nails and he hasn't got an ounce of feeling in him? He doesn't acknowledge the existence of romantic love—he doesn't even love Lara, if you think about it. He just wants to control her.'

'Oh, now I think that's going too far,' Rose put in. 'Of course he loves the girl. And he'll probably come round, given time. I hope so, anyway.'

'You hope in vain, Mother,' Janine said firmly.

'I learned very little from Lara,' Archie went on. 'About her family, I mean. I talked to her for almost half an hour on the phone and she spent most of that time just raving about her brother, telling me what a swine he is!' He laughed, obviously having taken it all with a pinch of salt.

'Well, you'd better believe it,' Janine said firmly, 'even if she is the dramatic type.'

'And prone to exaggeration, no doubt. Especially just now. After all, she's the injured party.'

So am I, Janine thought. She had taken personally Nikolai's insults about Robbie. And his insult in putting her in the servants' quarters could not be construed as anything other than personal. She had told her parents about that, and while her mother had been indignant, her father had roared with laughter. *Laughter!* 'Daddy, you're too nice. That's your trouble. You'd think the devil was misunderstood!'

She had spoken after a train of thought her father knew nothing about. Consequently he looked at her blankly, not understanding. 'Eh? Are you comparing Nikolai to the devil?'

'Not quite.' She flopped against the cushions of the armchair. She might just as well relax and get this over with. She would tell her parents everything Lara had told her about the Nekrassov family. Then they would know as much as she did about him—almost. And then she would make it clear she did not want to talk about the man ever again. 'Okay, Lara and Nikolai are of Russian descent, that much you know. The——'

'Is it true that Nikolai is a Count and Lara a Countess?' asked Rose, who found the idea fascinating for some reason.

'Technically, yes—of course. The father, Andrei, was taken to Paris by his father in 1917, during the Revolution. He was one year old. The grandfather, Piotr, was already a widower. He lost his wife, his land, his home, everything, as did thousands of others who were the aristocrats who fled—or were murdered. He was a displaced person who had a child to bring up and he was fortunate in getting a job in Paris, as a doorman outside a restaurant. He kept the job for years and years.

'Andrei grew up and became a *mechanicien*, a mechanic, and he later taught himself engineering. He worked as a mechanic during World War II, where he spent some time in England, fighting with the Free French.

'When he returned to France after the war, he passed through Lille, where he saw—and bought for a song—a run-down factory which had been gutted and looted. That was how Sabre Cars was first started, by Andrei, in a very small way to begin with, of course. Then he married a French girl, a local girl, and they had a son— Nikolai.

'Piotr was still working as a doorman in Paris. According to what Lara's been told, the old man was set in his ways and he refused to join Andrei and his family in Lille. They say he was afraid to change his life, even for the better.'

Archie grunted at that. 'After all he'd seen in life, I can understand that. He must have been dispirited, perhaps his spirit was broken after the Revolution and the comedown——'

'The comedown.' Janine picked up the phrase. 'Quite. It's hard for us to imagine the changes the grandfather lived through. And this is where the Nekrassov pride comes in. It seems Andrei *hated* the thought of his father working in a menial job. Piotr was dispirited, as you say, and he spent most of his time living in the past, living on old memories.

'Anyhow, by the early fifties, Andrei was starting to make money with his cars. But he didn't plough it back into the business, not at first. He sent Nikolai to a public school in England, determined to give the boy the best education money could buy. Then when he had made enough money, he bought the restaurant in Paris, the restaurant where his father had worked as doorman for donkey's years. He bought it *for* his father, lock, stock and barrel. Piotr was in his seventies by then; he owned the place for only five months before he died.'

'Good heavens . . .'

'Well!'

Janine smiled. It was an interesting story, there was no denying that. 'Yes, those must have been the best five months of the old man's life. From doorman to owner, what a kick it must have given him!'

'And Andrei. It must have been just as satisfying to him to see his father actually owning the restaurant. Perhaps more so, since he'd hated his father working as doorman.' Rose was smiling at the thought. 'What a sentimental streak Andrei had!'

'Sentimental?' Janine failed to see it.

'Of course. Doing somethng like that for his old dad! I think it's lovely.'

Janine was shaking her head. 'I don't think it had anything to do with sentiment. I think pride was the motivating factor, that Andrei was thumbing his nose at Paris, saying "See what I've done!" He did it for himself as much as anything else.'

'Well, I agree with your mother,' said Archie. 'I think it was an act of pure sentimentality, done wholly for the delight of old Piotr.' He paused to light his pipe again. 'So that's how Nikolai came to own the restaurant. I'd thought it rather incongruous that the owner of Sabre Cars should have a restaurant miles away from where he lives. Investing in bricks and mortar is one thing, but a restaurant? Anyhow, I take it the restaurant was passed back to Andrei when the old man died, and Andrei left it to Nikolai.'

'No, Piotr left it directly to Nikolai. No doubt this was done with Andrei's approval.'

'It was left to Nikolai? But surely he was just a lad?'

'Yes. He was ten years old. That's how long he's owned the place—twenty-five years. A manager was put in and Andrei had as little to do with the place as Nikolai has today.'

Her father smiled, his eyes narrowed thoughtfully. 'It's an interesting story, and they sound like an admirable family. I suppose Lara would have been co-owner, had she been around.'

'Probably. But she was born several years after the grandfather died. She says she was her parents' afterthought—or an accident! Dad, they don't sound like an admirable family to me. Except for Lara, who has the courage to stand against her brother with his outdated standards, his snobbery and all the atavistic programming he underwent.'

'Now what are you talking about?'

'It's true. Nikolai has told Lara of the stories he heard from his grandfather. I don't know any details, of course, but I've got the gist of it. It seems that Nikolai used to spend most of his school holidays with the old man in Paris. He adored him. They adored each other. As a boy, Nikolai was taught about his heritage, how the family once used to be great. Piotr lived in the past and he influenced the boy in his formative years. Lara thinks he shaped the boy's personality. She thinks this is why Nikolai is proud and power-mad.'

'Oh, Jan, really!' Archie looked positively disappointed now.

'Well, I believe it!' Janine was indignant then. 'How else do you explain Nikolai's attitudes and behaviour? Do you know, he actually wanted to choose her husband himself? Like they did in the old days! He had even told her *when* she could marry—after she'd finished her studies, of course. Lara told me.'

'Lara's told you a lot,' Archie sighed. 'Yet so little. There must be a hundred stories within the one she told you, a hundred possible interpretations which we could make about the Nekrassovs' actions. Everything I've heard is hearsay. Everything. Lara is too young to know anything first-hand.'

Janine got to her feet. 'If it's all the same to you, I'd rather drop the subject of Nikolai Nekrassov. For good.' She hedged slightly, seeing her father's look of curiosity. He didn't say anything, but she felt obliged to explain herself. 'I mean, there's no point in discussing him any more. Now I really must go to bed. I'm tired.'

There was a final question from her mother, however, before she left the room. 'Janine, do you think Lara will like Jersey? I do hope so. It would be so nice to have them living nearby!'

Janine smiled at her mother, understanding what she was hoping for. Robbie had worked in various countries for the past six years, Peter was in the Air Force and was stationed in Scotland, with his wife, and Janine was the only one who had come back to live on the island. But she, too, might well take off again. It was no secret that she felt unsettled; she had mentioned to her parents more than once that she might end up living in London. 'I don't think Lara's surroundings will matter much to her, Mum. If Robbie's inclined to settle here, then Lara will be. She's so much in love with him that I think she'd live on the dark side of the moon if he wanted her to! Goodnight, you two.'

As she stripped off and got into the bath, she was feeling disturbed because her father had made her realise she knew nothing about Nikolai, in spite of all she'd been told. Trust Archie to make her acknowledge that!

How much *had* Lara exaggerated—about everything? If her brother was really as bad as she made out, how was it she loved and respected him? What was Nikolai like, when he wasn't consumed with anger? Janine wondered. She would ask Lara when she saw her. There were all sorts of questions she wanted to ask about Nikolai . . .

It wasn't until she got out of the bath that she realised she was giving too much thought to the man, but this was probably because the memory of him was so fresh in her mind.

It certainly was fresh in her mind! And no, she didn't need to ask Lara anything. She had formed her *own* opinion of Nikolai Nekrassov and he was hateful, and Archie should take her word for that. She would not speak of him or even think of him again.

But she did think of him again, only a few minutes later when she caught sight of her naked body in her wardrobe mirror. She paused, nightie in hand, to look at her reflection. And all the determination in the world could not prevent the memories which flooded her mind. She got into bed, feeling nothing less than ashamed at the way she had allowed him to kiss her, at the way she had *responded*.

As things turned out, however, the name of Nikolai Nekrassov was not mentioned again in the Curtis house, much to Janine's satisfaction—and relief. When Lara and Robbie arrived the following week-end, which was the start of November, Lara flatly refused to speak of him. Rose and Archie complied; after all, there was nothing whatever to be gained by further discussions. It would have served only to compound Lara's distress. Besides, there were a great many other things to talk about, and plans to be made.

In spite of this Janine did not, could not, forget him. She tried, she tried very hard indeed, but as the weeks rolled by he crept into her thoughts a dozen times a day, like a nagging worry which had no foundation but refused to go away. She told herself this was due to Lara's presence in the house, the link she represented with Nikolai.

The memory of what he looked like didn't fade with time, either, as it should have done. When he was in her thoughts she had only to close her eyes and she could see him, she could see every detail of his face as if it were something she had known for years and years.

She knew this was strange. Again she told herself it was due to Lara's presence, that the striking resemblance to Nikolai was preventing the erosion of her vital memory of him. But that was not the truth of the matter, and in time she was forced to admit it.

In late November Lara and Robbie went back to Paris for a week in order to tie up the loose ends of the lives they had lived in France. They were going to settle down in Jersey. They would come back in a week, and prior to their wedding they would stay on with Archie and Rose while working on their cottage—that and several other things which would keep them occupied.

They did not rush into an immediate marriage, after all. After talking things over with Archie and Rose they decided to do things properly and to wait until the New Year, as they had originally planned. Their marriage was not going to be a hole-and-corner affair—far from it. And they would use the weeks in the meantime to prepare their home and to look around the island for suitable premises in which Robbie could open a restaurant of his own.

When they left for a week in late November, Janine felt guiltily relieved. She had already begun to love Lara, which wasn't a difficult thing to do, and could think of no one she would rather have as a sister-in-law. But she was relieved at the girl's absence because she had been a daily reminder of her brother, and she felt a sense of release.

However, Janine was not released. When Lara had been away for a few days she was forced to admit that. Nikolai came into her mind just as frequently, and when she closed her eyes she could still see him as plainly as ever. It really was as if the memory of him had been stamped on to her mind, never to be erased. And that irritated, oh, how it irritated! Worse than that, it frightened her a little. It was as if some faint but fundamental change had taken place in her, been forced upon her, and she knew it was not a change for the better. It was negative; something had been subtracted from her, a tiny part of her self had been stolen and she resented it beyond words. She cursed Nikolai for this, she cursd him for her own inability to forget him. She cursed him for existing at all until she realised the futility of what she was doing.

He would have forgotten her; she must do the same. She must. She would busy herself. She would date more often, with other men as well as with Michael Granger. The only way to combat negativity was with positivity.

She would broaden her circle of friends and acquaintances, and thereby occupy her time and her mind fully. This would force Nikolai Nekrassov from her thoughts and she would be whole again, no longer without that tiny part of her which seemed to have remained in a château in Lille.

CHAPTER FIVE

'IF you won't marry me, will you at least sleep with me?' Michael Granger took both her hands in his, his expression perfectly serious.

Janine searched his face, but in his eyes, eyes of a similar shade to her own, there was not even a hint of amusement. He meant what he said all right; the trouble was that she could not take him seriously. She never had been able to do that. She was about to make a flippant reply, but he went on.

'I want you, Janine. You have no idea how much I want you!' The grip on her hands tightened a little, the gesture and the force behind his words wiping the smile from her lips.

She looked at him even more closely, feeling slightly ill at ease. They were in a public place, though there was no danger of their being overheard. There were very few people in the bar—for the moment. Soon Robbie, Archie and her aunt and uncle from Bordeaux would be joining them and this disquieting conversation would stop.

It was the eve of Robbie's wedding, and they were in a hotel in Paris. Everyone but her and Michael had arrived the previous day. She and Michael had flown in that afternoon, and early tomorrow morning Peter and his wife would arrive from Scotland.

Today was the last Friday in January and everything was going beautifully. Everything had gone beautifully. Lara was already a part of the family as far as Janine and her parents were concerned. Rose treated her as if she were her own daughter—which in Rose's case did not mean treating her quite as an equal.

In getting to know Lara well, Janine had discovered her to be a curious mixture of woman and girl. Lara was nobody's fool; she was highly intelligent and quick-witted, able to talk with anyone on any level about anything. Nevertheless, she was only eighteen, and that part of her which was immature responded whole-heartedly to Rose's maternal instincts. Or perhaps it was simply that Lara enjoyed having a mother. It was something she had hardly known, her own mother having died when Lara was only four years old.

Rose had taught the girl the fundamentals of running a house, taught her basic cookery and even how to knit. In their respective roles as student and teacher, they delighted—which in turn delighted Robbie. The relationship between all concerned was good. During Christmas, when Peter and his wife had come to Jersey for three days, Lara had met the last of the Curtises.

Yes, everything was going beautifully, and Janine was immensely happy about it. Tomorrow afternoon Robbie and Lara would be married and leaving for a six-week honeymoon abroad—a wedding present from Archie and Rose.

At the moment Lara was staying at the home of a girl friend, and Rose was with her. This, out of respect for the superstition about the bride not seeing the groom on the eve of the wedding. Besides, Lara hadn't liked the idea of getting married from a hotel, but Robbie had long since given up his flat in Paris, of course.

The necessity of holding the wedding in Paris had proved to be expensive for Archie as well as an inconvenience. Still, without the necessary consent for Lara to marry in Jersey, there had been no choice in the matter. And Archie was footing all the bills—for the reception in the hotel, the plane fares and hotel expenses. He had insisted on doing this, although Robbie had wanteed to make at least a contribution.

A bachelor for many years, Robbie had substantial savings of his own. It was because of this, and his good standing with his bank in Jersey, that he had been able to get a loan for the restaurant he was buying. It was an established restaurant, not the empty premises they had originally been looking for to convert, though Robbie did intend to make considerable changes when he took over after his honeymoon.

'You might at least say something, Jan!' Michael laughed then, but it was more from anxiety than from amusement. 'I can't tell whether you're about to spit in my eye—or say yes to my suggestion!'

'I'm about to do neither,' she said quietly, even patiently. This was her own fault; in seeing more of Michael she had encouraged him even though she was not often alone with him. Michael moved in a clique, and she had allowed herself to be drawn into that clique in her determination to get out more and socialise. It was only occasionally that she had had dinner alone with Michael, but she had been careful not to mislead him into thinking she was interested in something more than friendship. In fact she had actually told him not to propose to her again, and she had even avoided kissing him goodnight.

But it seemed that her mild response to his suggestion was all the encouragement he needed. 'Let's stay in Paris for a few days,' he went on. 'Together. You're driving me crazy, don't you realise that? I love you, I want to marry you. It isn't just your body I want, but I'll settle for that if I can't have you for my wife.'

If he hadn't grinned on saying the last sentence Janine might, she just might, have taken him seriously. But she knew Michael Granger of old. She knew his current lifestyle, his past and even his future. Oh, he meant what he said. He did want to marry her; he would marry her. And he thought he loved her. But here was a man who really was suffering from an illusion. Here was a case where the emotion was unreal.

Michael Granger was tall, fair-haired, green-eyed, broad and good-looking. Janine thought him handsome. He was rich, he was charming and fun-loving. He played hard but he also worked hard. His family had established a chain of jewellery shops throughout the Channel Islands and Michael was heir to a great deal of money which had nothing to do with the shops—inherited money, from his father's side of the family. He didn't need to work, but he worked. He would not have been content to spend all his time playing. He was managing director in charge of the company and he did all the buying for the shops, as well as the overall management.

Acknowledging all his attributes did not help Janine to see him as a prospective husband or even as anything other than a brother. 'You know, Mike,' she said slowly, 'I know more about you than you know about yourself. I can name half a dozen women who would marry you tomorrow. Two of them are genuinely in love with you—you know who I'm referring to—and with them, your money doesn't enter into it.'

'Aw, thanks!' he interrupted, indignant. 'And the others would go along with it because I'm loaded, is that it? You don't take into account my vast experience as a lover and my irresistible personality! I don't know which charm school you've been to, but I don't think much of their teaching methods!'

She could not help laughing at him. 'Now let me finish.' She sobered. 'You know full well that you're the most eligible bachelor in Jersey. But in my opinion you're just not ready for marriage.'

'Darling, I'm thirty years old. How old do I have to be?'

'Stop interrupting, Michael. Age doesn't necessarily denote one's readiness for marriage. Think of the fun you have as a bachelor; do you honestly think you're ready to be faithful to one woman? Well, you're not. Not to this woman, anyhow.' She was smiling, pointing at herself. 'You've just got a bee in your bonnet about me. It all boils down to that old adage about forbidden fruit—you want me because I'm unavailable, that's all. If I were to be your lover, you'd use me as your latest plaything for a few months, then you'd move on to the next woman. And do you think it would be any different if I married you? What a disaster it would be!'

She was wrong, he thought. He had loved her for years. But he had already told her what a good foundation they had for marriage, in their very familiarity with one another. He wasn't going to say it again. Not now, not tonight. Nor would he give up. But for the moment he mustn't get too heavy. If he did, there would be a real danger of her refusing to see him again.

So Michael just smiled and shook his head, telling her she was incorrigible but delightful with it. Then he changed the subject as he saw Robbie and Archie coming into the bar. 'Hey, here's the groom-to-be! I'm not sure whether, in my capacity as best man, I should encourage or discourage his drinking tonight!'

Janine turned round and waved to the newcomers, her conversation with Michael already forgotten. He was a lot of fun to be with and even when he waxed romantic it gave her a laugh. She had, of course, absolutely no wish to hurt him in any way, but the fact that he took her refusals—all of them—so lightly demonstrated that what he felt for her was only surface-deep.

The church was small, very old and beautiful. Janine and her parents stepped into its shadowy coolness and sat quietly, watching everyone else take their places. Robbie was already there, and Michael, and within five minutes Lara's friends were seated. Not that there were many of them—a fact which saddened Janine rather. And of course there were no relatives present to see her get married. As far as Lara knew, she only had one.

Janine looked down at her hands, only vaguely aware of the soft strains of the church organ. Not once had Lara mentioned his name. In all these weeks, not once. But how was she feeling now? Happy, of course. But her happiness must surely be tinged with sorrow.

Glancing at her watch, Janine saw that Lara should be arriving now, precisely now. She hoped against hope that the weather was holding out, her eyes travelling to the beautiful old windows for signs of rain. The afternoon sky was heavily overcast, threatening an imminent downpour. But so far it was holding off, casting greyness over the streets of Paris.

She saw her mother smile with something approaching relief at the exact moment that the music changed, and she turned to see Lara at the end of the short aisle, looking very, very beautiful. Her hand was resting on the arm of her girl friend's father, a middle-aged man who looked suitably pleased to be filling the role which actually belonged to someone else.

Determinedly, Janine pushed the thought from her mind; nothing must spoil this day, not even an errant thought. This day must be perfect, for Robbie and Lara.

When next she looked at her mother, the ceremony had begun. Rose's eyes were full of tears, in her hand there was a neatly folded lace handkerchief which would no doubt be soaked by the time her son was married. She had left Lara only half an hour earlier, having helped to dress her and calm her, no doubt. So Janine had had no chance to talk with her mother and enquire the extent of the bride's nervousness.

If Lara was nervous, it didn't show in her voice. She and Robbie spoke clearly in voices which reached the back of the church. Janine looked on, totally absorbed by what she was hearing and seeing as the minutes ticked by.

Then, quite suddenly, inexplicably, the face of Nikolai Nekrassov floated into her vision. It was two-dimensional, as if it were superimposed on what she was actually seeing. She blinked rapidly, willing it to go away, telling herself it had been invoked by the thoughts she had had prior to the ceremony starting.

Then just as suddenly, just as inexplicably she knew he was there, in the flesh. She could feel his presence. An icy shiver ran down her spine and she turned slowly, almost dreading having her knowledge confirmed.

He was there.

He was standing just inside the doors of the church, immaculate in a dark suit and tie, a white shirt. His eyes were fixed on the bride and groom. He looked neither pleased nor displeased, rather as if ... merely as if he were concentrating.

Janine felt as if the pit of her stomach had dropped.

For seconds the fine lines of his face moved out of focus as her heart galloped so furiously she could hear the blood pounding against her ears. Had she not been sitting, she would have fallen. The shock of this was unlike anything she had experienced before.

She could feel the colour draining from her face, knew that she must turn away from what she was seeing if she were to hang on to her composure. All of this took place in mere seconds. As the thought crossed her mind, her eyes closed and opened again at once. But this was no trick of the imagination or her eyes. It was no illusion. He was there, and at the instant she started to turn away, Nikolai's indigo eyes flicked rapidly to hers, and held.

For split seconds they held, but only for split seconds. Janine turned away as quickly as she dared without attracting attention, without provoking so much as a glance from her father, who was seated to her right.

On Archie's right was Rose, dabbing delicately at her eyes with the lacy hanky, oblivious to anything but her son and his new wife. And Lara was Robbie's wife now. It was all over. Janine was aware of that much, but nothing else. In the ensuing minutes she sat motionless and sick with fear. Nikolai was here to cause trouble. There could be no other reason. But how did he know where the wedding was to take place? How did he know *when* it was to take place? There had been no contact from him whatsoever.

She wasn't seeing or hearing anything now. Nikolai was too late to prevent the marriage. It didn't make sense. Nothing made sense except the obvious: he was here to create a scene, to spoil this the most important day of his sister's life. The bastard! She shut her eyes, anticipating the look of horror on Lara's face when she caught sight of Nikolai.

'Janine. Janine!'

She swallowed hard, feeling sick as she became aware of the quiet urgency in her father's voice. What was happening? What had Archie seen? What was Nikolai doing now?

Archie was leaning close, his voice no more than a whisper. 'What's wrong? What is it? Lord, you look as if you've seen a ghost! You're as white as a sheet!'

A ghost? Oh, no! she wanted to say. She might have handled that better, she wanted to say. But she couldn't say anything at all. Instead she just looked into her father's eyes and then turned around in her seat, willing him to do likewise. It didn't occur to her that he wouldn't recognise Nikolai Nekrassov. She was concerned only with warning her father of the trouble which lay ahead.

But Nikolai had gone.

Her mouth opened and closed stupidly as her father turned her round, his hand under her elbow. 'What on earth's the matter, Jan? What *is* it?'

'N-Nikolai is here,' she managed, turning again to look. 'That is, he was here.'

Archie turned again, and to her horror she saw he was smiling. Dear God, didn't her father understand anything? Why was he looking *pleased*?

But Archie's look of pleasure was fleeting. He shrugged, looking at Janine uncertainly. 'I don't see anybody. Anyhow, not a word about this to anyone now—including your mother. Do you hear?'

She heard him. Just. For the moment she would do as he asked. After all, what else could she do? Shout out to the whole congregation?

Nothing out of place happened during the following hour, an hour which seemed like an eternity to Janine. Throughout the photographic session and during the drive back to the hotel, her eyes were everywhere. She was waiting for Nikolai to reappear, dreading the thought that he might already be at the hotel, waiting for everyone's arrival before he said what he wanted to say and ruined the entire day.

Her worries came to nothing. The reception went beautifully without even the smallest hitch. The perfect day was unspoiled for everyone except Janine, who spent the afternoon and evening in a state of nervous anxiety she hid very successfully. It was only when the newlyweds left for the airport and their six-week honeymoon that she had a chance to speak to her father alone.

'You *what?*' She and Archie were standing in a corner of the large reception room, out of earshot. It was just as well nobody was paying attention to them, because the look on her face was one of incredulity. 'Dad, you're telling me you sent Nikolai an invitation to the wedding? But why? *Why?*'

'Now that's a daft question.' Archie spoke as if he couldn't understand the fuss she was making. 'It was worth a try, wasn't it?'

'What are you talking about?' she snapped, actually angry with her father and not afraid to show it. Her respect for him was enormous, but she couldn't understand what had made him behave so thoughtlessly.

'A reconciliation, of course. What else? I thought it might do the trick.'

Janine floundered, speechless. 'I—you—didn't you stop to think of the dangers in letting him know where and when the wedding was to take place?'

'What dangers?' He honestly didn't know what she was fussing about.

'The havoc he could have caused!'

'But he didn't . . .'

'The way he could have upset Lara!'

'But he didn't . . .'

'You had no right, Daddy! You had no right to take it upon yourself to——'

'But I didn't. Heavens above, girl, will you calm down? What's got into you?' Placing a hand on her shoulder, he shook her slightly. 'Listen to me. It was my idea, yes. But I discussed it with Robbie, naturally. He and I decided it was worth a try, sending the invitation. He—we both hoped Nikolai would come along and *make* Lara's day, not ruin it.'

'Then you're both shortsighted.' Janine was adamant, but her father could not be convinced.

He sighed. 'At least he turned up to watch the ceremony. I'd hoped for more than that, but his putting in an appearance is some encouragement.'

It was no use being angry with him. Their thinking was so diverse on the subject of Nikolai that Janine knew she wouldn't change his mind. Which did not stop her from saying what she thought. 'Father dear, I'll say this once—just once. Nikolai Nekrassov did *not* turn up for sentimental reasons. He went to that church expecting to find Robbie abandoned, he was so convinced Lara would not defy him. Believe me. He was waiting to say, "I told you so" to Robbie, to me, to all of us.'

'What nonsense! After all this time? Had Lara been going to change her mind, she'd have done it before today—and Nikolai knew that. Granted, he might be too proud to bury the hatchet, but he wasn't there to cause trouble. He was there purely and simply to watch his sister get married.'

That was how it appeared, Janine couldn't deny that. In view of Nikolai's vanishing act when the ceremony was over, Archie must be forgiven for deluding himself. But Janine knew better. She slipped her hand through her father's arm and led him in the direction of a group of people. The subject was finished. She would not speak of it again.

Nor did she speak of it again. Neither did Archie, not with her. But it took a long time for Janine to get over that day in Paris. She had to try all over again to sublimate to a tolerable degree the way Nikolai infiltrated her thoughts. Not that she had succeeded in doing this when she had first tried to, in spite of the distractions she had given herself.

She and Rose stayed in Paris for a few days and did some shopping. They returned to Jersey to a home that was normal again inasmuch as there were just the three of them. The honeymooners knew nothing of Nikolai's brief appearance at their wedding, but Archie told Rose about it and she, too, was pleased, seeing it as an encouraging sign—just as her husband did. Janine made no comment at all.

So Nikolai was being spoken of again—and her resentment of him doubled. It had nothing to do with

Lara now; Nikolai could not hurt her any more, or any more than he had already. She was married and living her own life.

No, Janine's resentment was purely personal because he had some inexplicable hold over her which she could not shake off. Seeing him again, albeit very briefly, had made it impossible for her to forget him.

Two weeks after the wedding she was still feeling disturbed at the memory of how she had *felt* his presence in the church. Over and over she told herself it had been just a fluke, that she had just happened to think of him seconds before she turned and saw him. But she could not convince herself of this, and as a consequence she felt deeply unsettled within herself. She felt as if she were no longer her own person. And that rankled. If only she had never gone to Lille! If only she had not allowed Robbie to talk her into it . . .

Things took a turn for the worse in the middle of the following week. From Janine's point of view, at least. The episode resulted in her having another argument with her father—an argument she was bound to lose.

It was Wednesday, almost three weeks after the wedding. Janine was in the travel agency and things were pretty quiet. Archie had taken the morning off to play golf—something he did often these days not only because things were quiet, being out of season, but also because he felt entitled, quite rightly, to take things easier at his age.

He came to work just after two o'clock and found his daughter in his private office, above the shop. She threw away her sandwich wrappings and smiled at him. 'Hi! Good game?'

'Good game. Very good.' Archie sank into a chair and took the cup of tea she handed to him. 'I won. Played two under my handicap to boot!'

Janine looked suitably impresssed. She swam a lot, played tennis and went horse riding, but golf had never appealed to her.

Without preamble, Archie delivered his news. 'Look, at this.' He fished in his pocket and drew out a white envelope. 'It came this morning. I reckon you owe me an apology, young lady. It's a letter from Nikolai Nekrassov. Read it.'

Janine was dumbstruck. A letter? And her father's remark about an apology implied that it contained good news—from his point of view. She almost snatched the envelope from him, angry even before she read the letter. The envelope contained not only a short letter but also a cheque, a cheque for a substantial amount of money. She stared briefly at the cheque before reading what Nikolai had to say.

There was very little to his explanation. He was sending the money to cover the 'considerable' expenses incurred by the wedding, he said. As the bride's brother and guardian, he acknowledged that it was his 'duty' to pay for the wedding. 'Duty?' Janine picked on that particular word. 'See that, Dad? His duty! And what about the rest of his *duties*?'

She glanced once more at the missive before stuffing it and the cheque back into the envelope. It was handwritten with a fountain pen using black ink. The strokes of the pen were strong and positive, a stark contrast against the white paper, which was, of course, of the finest quality. The address of the château was printed at the top in black, the lettering bold and without fuss, just like Nikolai's writing.

Janine thrust the envelope towards her father, who had said nothing. 'Send this back to him and tell him to go to hell. Tell him you don't need his lousy money.'

Archie sat very still, looking at her thoughtfully. After several seconds he shook his head, almost sadly. 'He's offering the olive branch and you want me to throw it back in his face?'

'Olive branch?' Janine shook her head in disbelief, repeating the words. 'He isn't offering the olive branch! He's trying to appease his conscience by sending you a cheque!'

'Can't you read between the lines?' Archie asked quietly.

'There is nothing between the lines,' Janine said stubbornly. 'Nothing but emptiness. Cold white space.'

'You know very well what I mean, Jan.' It was as if

her father had made up his mind to remain absolutely patient with her. 'I've had several hours in which to think about this,' he went on, tapping his forefinger against the envelope. 'And I know exactly how I'm going to reply to it.'

Janine got up and poured herself a cup of tea. She could hardly look at her father; she didn't want to know in what vein he was going to reply. How could she convince him that Nikolai Nekrassov was best ignored? 'Don't,' she said harshly, 'please don't accept that cheque. Don't let him pay for his bad behaviour with a cheque! It's too easy for the likes of him, don't you see? Don't you see?' She turned to find her father filling his pipe. This was so much a part of what he was, something she had witnessed a thousand times before, but it suddenly irritated her so much that she wanted to shake him. 'I asked you a question!'

Archie shrugged. 'I'm not going to keep the cheque.'

Letting out a long breath released some of Janine's tension. Thank goodness for that, she thought and then voiced the thought.

'I shall write and say it was my pleasure to pay for my son's wedding. I shall tell him Lara is a most welcome member of our family. I'll thank him for writing and say I hope to meet him one day, that he's welcome in my home any time he cares to come.' Archie was using a finger to pack the tobacco into his pipe. When he had finished he took out his lighter, watching his daughter's face as he lit up. 'Now what?'

'I'll tell you.' Janine's mouth set stubbornly. She would tell her father how Robbie got his black eye and sprained wrist; that would change his mind, that would stop him being so infuriatingly neutral and patient. Oh, she wasn't worried about Nikolai turning up in Jersey; there would be no danger of that. It was more than the man's pride would allow.

But he wasn't the only one with pride; as an injured party Janine was entitled to hers, and she couldn't bear to think of such a pleasant response being given to that curt, formal and meaningless letter. 'Robbie didn't get his black eye and damaged wrist by falling down some

steps, like he told you. He lied, and I went along with
the lie for Mummy's sake, knowing how upset she'd be
if she knew the truth. So did Lara.' She watched
Archie's face as she spoke, unable to keep the
satisfaction from her voice. 'Nikolai Nekrassov was the
real cause. He turned physically vicious on Robbie that
Sunday in Lille. He punched your son and sent him
sprawling. Now perhaps you'll understand my attitude.'

That Archie had flinched on hearing what happened
gave her added satisfaction. 'Why did he do that? There
must be a reason.'

'Of course there was a reason! It was his way of
telling Robbie what he thought of his wanting to marry
Lara! Now do you see the type of person we're dealing
with?' She waited expectantly in the face of her father's
silence, knowing a twinge of conscience because she
hadn't told the whole truth.

Nor was she going to tell the whole truth, and when
Archie pressed her for more information, she just
repeated what she had said. But Archie Curtis already
knew what had provoked the violence. At least, he
knew what Lara had said in desperation. Now he put
two and two together. 'Well, Jan, I can't say it's the
way I would have reacted, had I been told someone had
got you into trouble when you were eighteen, but I can
understand it.'

Janine's heart sank. She knew then that she had lost.
It seemed unnecessary to comment about Lara's stupid
lie, but she did. 'So Lara told you what she'd said about
being pregnant.'

'On the phone, when she was all upset. She poured it
all out—apart from the bit about the punch. You know
how outspoken she is.'

Janine sat on the edge of the desk and said nothing.

Sighing, Archie brought an end to the discussion with
a short speech followed by a solitary question. 'I heard
a lot of ranting over the telephone from Lara. I heard a
lot of ranting from you when you came back after
meeting Nikolai. Bear in mind that everyone's emotions
were running high at that time, that all we ever wanted
was for Lara's brother to be reasonable. Well, he's

being reasonable now. My returning his cheque will
show him I'm not impressed by money. I hope he reads
between the lines of *my* letter. If he makes a personal
visit, then I'll be impressed. For now, I'll continue to
keep an open mind.

'As for you, Jan ... you tried to persuade me into
thinking he would never bury the hatchet. You were
wrong. I've never known you think and behave so
illogically—look at the suggestion you gave me today!
You want me to tell him to go to hell, when a
reconciliation is just around the corner? Really, Jan!
For some obscure reason, your thinking has become
warped. I can only conclude that there's something you
haven't told me. Something *else* you're keeping from
me. So what is it. What happened between you and
Nikolai that's made you hate him like this?'

His reasoning should not have come as a shock to
her, but it did. Of course it was typical of him to sift out
the truth, to ask the reasons why a person behaved the
way they did. He had taught Janine to be like that
herself—Janine and his other children. 'I've told you,'
she said dully. 'I told you about that business with the
servants' quarters. I told you I think him despicable.'

Archie gave her an oblique look. 'That's not good
enough. Is there anything else?'

Of course there was something else; her inability to
forget the Frenchman's kiss, her inability to rid him
completely from her thoughts. But she couldn't tell her
father of these things, and the realisation *why* she
couldn't brought a wave of fear in its wake.

How very complicated this was. No, no, it was
perfectly simple. If she told Archie the whole truth, he
would want to know why she was so affected ... and
that was something Janine had been avoiding asking
herself.

She would continue to avoid it, too. It was something
she dared not think about. She got off the desk and told
her father she was going out for a walk. As she left the
office, he had already taken out Nikolai's letter. No
doubt he intended replying there and then.

Janine closed the door softly. Let Archie do as he

wished; not that she could stop him. There was, she supposed, the possibility of a reply from Nikolai. A reply to the reply. She had to acknowledge that possibility now. But she would not acknowledge the possibility of Nikolai accepting Archie's invitation. She dreaded that thought so much that she wouldn't even consider it as feasible.

But Nikolai did come to Jersey. He came two weeks later, without prior warning. Without so much as a phone call or a note in advance, he turned up at the Curtis home on a Sunday morning—the last Sunday of the newlyweds' honeymoon.

CHAPTER SIX

JANINE was away, too. She had gone to London for a couple of days. She left after work on the Saturday evening and spent two days with a girl friend, an old school friend, in her flat in West London.

Pauline Norris had moved from Jersey to London after she had been jilted about a year earlier—a few months after Janine had come back from working in Switzerland. They had always kept in touch and continued to do so, taking it in turns to visit every few months, and have a good natter.

Janine had felt very much in need of a natter, or rather a confidential talk with Pauline, whom she trusted absolutely. She had taken the short flight to the mainland with every intention of telling her friend all about Nikolai Nekrassov—the whole story. Yet she had said not a word about him, for reasons she couldn't fathom.

But she had told Pauline how unsettled she felt at home, and Pauline had said she was welcome to move in with her if she decided to leave Jersey. The flat had two bedrooms, so there was no problem, and it was handy for the Underground station, too, Pauline had added persuasively. And there was plenty of temp work around in London from Easter onwards.

Janine had thanked her friend for the offer but had not committed herself; she really couldn't decide what to do. She had the feeling that moving to London would not of itself be the answer to—whatever it was that ailed her.

She had left her car at the airport on Jersey and she drove home in no particular hurry, thinking mainly of Michael and the party his family were giving on Friday. It would be a sumptuous affair indeed, and today was Monday. She would have to buy something pretty spectacular to wear and she had left it till the last minute, which wasn't like her.

Driving through St Helier, she decided against taking a quick look around the shops now. It was four o'clock—too late. She would need half a day to find the right thing. Perhaps her father would let her take Wednesday morning off? Today was an official day off because she had worked Saturday, but Archie would no doubt give her Wednesday morning, too. It certainly had its advantages, being the boss's daughter!

The party was being held by the Grangers as a celebration of their having been in business for twenty-five years. Friday would be twenty-five years to the day when Michael's father opened his first jewellery shop on the island. How the business had grown; they had a string of shops throughout the Channel Islands now.

Janine was half a mile from home when the feeling of unease stole over her. She found herself braking for no reason, much to the annoyance of the man in the car to her rear. She let him pass, having slowed her own car to a crawl, her concentration distracted by the uncomfortable feeling that something was wrong at home. Then she put her foot on the acclerator and carried on at a normal place, determinedly shaking off the feeling because it was illogical.

But it wasn't illogical. The Curtis house was big and old, its gardens surrounded by a six-foot brick wall, so Janine didn't see the visitor's car until she had actually turned into the drive. And there it was, Nikolai's car, long and sleek and white, a masterpiece of engineering and comfort combined, gleaming in the fading March light.

Driving past it and into the double garage where her father's car was parked, Janine had the incongruous thought that Nikolai would have to drive a Sabre car for the rest of his life. How could he drive anything else? Not that that presented any hardship!

She didn't mind having to face him, she didn't mind either that her father had been right all along. What she minded was the weird occurrence which had taken place half a mile down the road. It was different from but reminiscent of the way she had sensed Nikolai's presence that day in the church in Paris. But she could not explain these incidents—she didn't even try.

As she let herself into the house she stopped dead in the hallway, hearing Nikolai's voice coming from the living room. It was only then that the shock set in, only then that the reality of his presence really hit her. And how it hit her! It was like a physical blow, just as it had been in the church.

Her heart was racing now just as it had raced then and she felt as though her legs were suddenly paralysed. She didn't even attempt to move; she just stood, trying to rationalise what was happening to her. There had been a rational explanation in church, when she had been able to attribute her strange physical reaction on seeing Nikolai to her fear that he was going to cause havoc. But now? Now there was no such worry; he was obviously here to make peace, so why was she reacting like this when there was nothing to be afraid of?

Because she hated him, that was why. And she resented what the sound of his voice could do to her, she resented the way he had haunted her mind ever since the day she had met him. She wished fervently that he had not come to Jersey—regardless of Lara.

Regardless of Lara? What was she thinking about? She ought to be rejoicing now, not willing Nikolai to go away!

What an invidious position she was in! She had, of course, no choice but to make an attempt at friendliness—as her mother and father were obviously doing. Moving closer to the living room door, Janine listened for a moment. Yes, it all sounded very friendly indeed, and she would have to act accordingly, for the sake of her sister-in-law.

Janine squared her shoulders and tried to compose herself. For Lara's sake, she would forget her own hatred of the man and make an effort. She put down her week-end case (which she had held on to all this time), and opened the door to the living room.

Quite what happened to her then, she didn't know. So many impressions and emotions hit her that she forgot her good resolution under their onslaught. She took in the scene with a swift sweep of her eyes, saying an automatic hello to her parents, who were on the sofa, a tray of tea and cakes on the low table before them.

And there was Nikolai, sitting in an armchair with his long legs stretched out before him. Dressed casually in a white polo-neck sweater and plain slacks, he seemed perfectly relaxed and at ease, while she ... she was forced to acknowledge all over again how strikingly, intensely attractive he was. Not that she had forgotten! She had not been able to forget, dammit! But the impact of his appearance was a hundred times more powerful now he was actually in her home rather than in her mind.

Perhaps it was this which brought out her aggression. Perhaps it was the impassive look on his aristocratic face, a look that held not the slightest interest or curiosity, which angered her and made her feel strangely disappointed at the same time. Or maybe it was that way he had of holding his head—the unmistakable arrogance about it. That, and the unpleasant memories it provoked of their row. Whatever, Janine reacted without so much as a thought for reconciliation. 'Well, well,' she said facetiously, 'if it isn't the Russian Count! What are you doing here, Nikolai Andreivitch, mixing with the proleteriat?'

'Janine!' The word came simultaneously from Archie and Rose, but she ignored it, not taking her eyes from Nikolai.

'A little infra dig, isn't it?' she demanded, gesturing towards the coffee table. 'Taking tea with the bourgeoisie!'

'That's *enough*!' Archie's voice came out so furiously that she could not fail to be affected by it, it was so out of character. Her father's anger and disappointment were written all over his face, and her mother had paled noticeably.

They were right. They were right to be angry and disappointed in her. What had she been thinking about in attacking him like that? Not Lara, that was for sure. Oh, how far removed from consideration for Lara Janine's thoughts had been! But she didn't want Nikolai here, she didn't want him to be in Lara's life because it would inevitably put him on the periphery of her own life.

Only then did she realise this, and how selfish it was. She *had* to make an effort. For Lara and Robbie, for her parents, for the sake of peace. She turned to Nikolai again, not quite meeting his eyes. 'I'm sorry.' It came out very quietly because the words almost stuck in her throat.

'What was that, Janine? I didn't hear you.' Nikolai's voice could not have been more neutral, but she knew he was laughing at her.

She fixed her eyes on his, hating him and knowing that it showed. 'I said I'm sorry.' Her voice was loud now, loud and brittle. He had heard her the first time, of course. His indigo eyes were openly laughing at her now and her outburst had not perturbed him in the least.

'I'll get a cup for you, Jan.' Rose got to her feet. 'Give me your coat.'

Janine handed her coat to her mother and sat down with as much dignity as she could muster. Here she was, on her own territory, being laughed at by Nikolai Nekrassov and unable to fight back because she was obliged to consider others.

Her father was looking at her expectantly now and she was well aware that he was still angry—a rare occurrence indeed. She was obliged, Archie was obliging her, to talk to Nikolai, to say something polite, to make conversation with him. Knowing it wouldn't be easy, she tried. 'I—how long have you been here? I assume you've been told the newlyweds are still on honeymoon?'

'Yes.' He smiled then, but it did not reach his eyes. 'It never occurred to me they'd be away so long. I naturally assumed they'd be here—on the island, I mean. I came yesterday to introduce myself to your parents and to ask for their address.'

'Yesterday?' Janine was surprised at that. 'So where are you staying? Or rather, why are you staying? Your sister won't be back until Saturday afternoon.'

'Nikolai is aware of that.' That Archie did not like her line of questioning was obvious in his voice. 'And he's staying here, of course. He's in no hurry to go back to France, so he's staying here until Robbie and Lara come home.'

Janine's heart sank, but she tried, and succeeded, in keeping the dismay from her face.

Rose came in with a cup and saucer just as Nikolai spoke. 'I intend to look around the island while I'm here, which is the reason I brought my car over. This is my first visit to Jersey, you know.' His tone was casual, conversational, but his eyes were laughing at her again—though she was the only one who was aware of it. 'I had in fact booked a suite at the Hotel de France, but your parents insisted I stay here. I hope it's okay with you?'

Oh, how he was enjoying putting her on the spot! 'Of course,' she said, looking not at him but at her father.

But Archie had not forgiven her yet and things got worse for Janine. 'I've told our guest that I'm giving you the week off work, Jan. Keep Nikolai company and show him our island. I reckon you know the place better than any of us.' This was accompanied by a smile, but the slight stress on the word 'guest' had not gone unnoticed. Her father was warning her not to argue about it.

She did argue, albeit half-heartedly. A week of Nikolai's company was the last thing she wanted. She had to make some protest! 'But I can't really be spared from work, Dad. I mean, we're getting busy now Easter's coming and——'

'We'll cope,' Archie said flatly. 'It's time you had a break in any case.'

Quite what that was supposed to mean, Janine didn't know. She looked appealingly at her mother, but if Rose was aware of all the undercurrents, it didn't show. 'Nikolai wants to take you out to dinner tonight, darling,' Rose said. 'I told him you'd be happy to cook something here for him but he thought you might not be in the mood after your journey.'

'But why?' Janine blurted. 'Where are you going?'

'It's Monday.' The answer came from Archie and he said it as if she should have known better than to ask. 'The second Monday of the month, too.'

Bridge. Archie and his wife played bridge every Monday evening. And on the second Monday of every month there was a competition. So he and Rose would not have been able to avoid their commitment even if they had wanted to—which they didn't.

Janine was cornered, well and truly cornered.

'Perhaps Janine has a date?' Nikolai put in, watching her as closely as he had watched her throughout all this. He was enjoying her discomfiture, of that she was certain.

She looked at him levelly, realising that she had to put a stop to this. The tension was tangible between herself and her father, herself and Nikolai, and it was getting on her nerves. Between them they had sewn up her time for the rest of the week—except for Friday. On Friday night she was going to the Grangers' party and she was damned if she would take Nikolai with her! She would mention it now, thus giving her parents warning that they would have the Frenchman to themselves on Friday, at least.

The trouble was that Archie and Rose had as much in common with their guest as she did—absolutely nothing. All right, she could understand their inviting him to stay in the house, since he was going to stay on the island in any case. But they were fobbing him off on her, and she was furious about it! It wasn't fair! They *knew* how she felt about the wretched man.

With a monumental effort she said casually, 'No, I haven't got a date. Not tonight. But I have a date on Friday evening and I've planned on shopping on Wednesday morning, but apart from that my time is yours, Nikolai.'

He inclined his head slightly, his eyes dancing with laughter. 'I'm honoured. How very nice!'

'Good.' Archie finally relaxed and gave her a smile. Boy, would she have a few things to say to her father when she got him alone! How *could* he manoeuvre her like this?

But of course he could. And it wasn't a question of manoeuvring. He expected her to do her duty, that was all. And to keep her feelings out of it. The irritating thing was that he was right, too. He was acting from the best possible motives.

Janine sighed inwardly, feeling trapped, stymied. She drained her teacup and got to her feet. 'Will you excuse me now?' she said to the room at large. 'I'm feeling a little crumpled after my journey and I'd like to take a bath.'

Nikolai actually stood up as she left the room, a faint smile playing around his mouth as he watched her go. It served nicely to detract from the courteous gesture he had made in standing and it was, of course, designed to irritate her. She shot him a look of pure hatred as she closed the living room door.

What a gift he had for being sarcastic without needing to open his mouth! Janine took the stairs two at a time, frustrated beyond description. But not for long. Oh, no, this would last only until she was alone with him!

She locked herself in the bathroom, which was not en-suite to her bedroom but which she would not have to share with Nikolai. Her parents had an en-suite bathroom, but there were two more in the house—one of which was hers and the other of which had been her brothers'.

Thank goodness for small mercies, she thought. She

could have a long soak without having to worry about his needing the bathroom. Her mind was racing. Nikolai Nekrassov was a total mystery to her now. She had not expected this visit. First he had appeared at the wedding, then he had sent a cheque in payment of all expenses and now he was here, to make peace with his sister. Janine would never have believed it. She had been convinced he would carry out his threat and rid Lara from his life. What had changed his mind? She would ask him over dinner. That question and a dozen others.

She would also tell him a few things, too. Until she was alone with him, she could not be herself. Her position was indeed an awkward one; in her parents' presence she was obliged to hold her tongue, but she would do no such thing when she was alone with Nikolai. She would tell him precisely what she thought of him on a personal level, and that would have nothing to do with family matters!

Flicking through the contents of her wardrobe an hour later, Janine felt calmer. She had washed and dried her hair and it was behaving beautifully. It mattered, too. It mattered that she looked just right this evening because it was going to be something of an ordeal and she needed all the confidence she could give herself. So she had made up with care, not too little, not too much, and the dress she planned on wearing was one in which she always felt good.

It was a red coat-dress, belted and straight in the skirt. It was just the right thing for a cool, March evening, though possibly not quite dressy enough for dining in a restaurant. But that would depend on the restaurant. She glanced at her watch as she went downstairs, wondering where to suggest they should eat. It was early; there would be no need to book in advance at this time of the evening, not in March.

Nikolai was having a drink with her parents. He had changed and was now wearing a light grey suit with a white shirt which made a stark contrast against the tan of his skin. It crossed Janine's mind that he must have spent some time in the sun since she first met him, because his skin tone was even darker than she remembered. He was the sort of person who tanned very easily, and it emphasised the intense blueness of his eyes.

Those eyes moved over her slowly as she walked into the room, showing interest now, and approval, although he made no comment about her appearance. 'Rose was just telling me she's half-French,' he said. 'You never mentioned there was French blood in the family.'

Janine smiled at him. 'You never asked,' she said sweetly. 'I'm ready if you are. Shall we go? I thought we'd eat in a hotel, if that's all right with you. How about the one you mentioned earlier? It's one of the best on the island.'

Nikolai drained his glass and they bade Rose and Archie goodnight and good luck with their game. It would be hours before her parents came home, she thought suddenly. Invariably they spent a few hours socialising after bridge. The thought made her nervous; it meant she would find herself alone in the house with Nikolai, unless she could think of somewhere else to take him after they had eaten . . .

But it was just as bad being alone with him in his car. As soon as they were ensconced in the small space, his nearness affected her unreasonably and she tensed, sitting as far away from him as possible.

Nothing was said until they got on to the road at the bottom of the drive, when Nikolai broke the silence. 'I'm relying on you for directions, Janine . . . and may I say I approve your choice of perfume. Dior, isn't it?'

She set about him at once, her cool and composure nonexistent. 'Turn left. And spare me the compliments! Insincerity is tantamount to lying! You can be yourself now we no longer have an audience. As I can. So let me tell you right now that I don't want to dine with you, I don't want to spend several days showing you around the island, I don't want you in my home—what are you doing?'

He had brought the car to a halt and was switching off the engine. 'Giving you my undivided attention.' He turned to face her, his arm resting on the steering wheel. For the first time ever, she saw him smile properly; it reached his eyes, it changed his entire countenance and it infuriated Janine as much as it fascinated her.

He was beautiful, no less. He was also highly amused by her outburst. 'So tell me something I don't already know,' he said. 'For example, do your eyes always sparkle so delightfully when you're angry, or is it the lamplight?'

'Stop it!' She looked away, disturbed because she found herself wishing he meant what he had said. 'Drop the act, Nikolai. It won't work. Charm doesn't suit you.'

'But you said I can be myself now we're alone,' he protested, his deep voice rather than his eyes mocking her now. 'And I'm really very nice—once you get to know me. So why don't we start afresh and get to know one another? Why don't you show a little friendliness and tolerance to this new member of your family?'

She glared at him. 'Very clever! I have no choice but to tolerate you—for my parents' sake. You know damned well the awkward position I'm in. They are delighted at your change of heart, delighted you've come around. But you're an unknown quantity at the moment—they fear you'll sail back to France in a huff if I openly show my animosity towards you.'

He was further amused by that. 'So you're showing me in private.'

'Right.'

'But you're prepared to tolerate me for the sake of others?'

'I don't see that I have a choice.' She turned away from him. 'Personally I find you despicable.'

'I'm sorry you feel like this,' he said quietly, the amusement gone from his voice. 'And it's ironic. After all, it's because of you that I'm here.'

'Because of me?' Janine looked at him suspiciously. His words had jolted her because for an instant she had misunderstood. She had thought he meant he was there because of her *personally*. Surely he didn't actually mean that?

Of course he didn't. 'It was that little speech you gave me,' he explained. 'I thought about it a great deal. I began to see the sense in some of the things you said.'

So Nikolai was here because of the things she had said to him! Her anger towards him lessened a little. How could she help feeling satisfied, even flattered, to hear that? 'Then why did it take you so long to make contact? Your pride, I suppose. You had to swallow your pride.'

'No,' he said quietly, considering. 'Actually, no. I didn't make contact until after the wedding because up to the last moment I was still convinced that Lara would not marry your brother.'

'But——'

'Be quiet,' he said firmly, all mockery and amusement gone. 'There are several things we have to clear up between us. Hear me out. Think how it looked to me. Lara was fresh out of school, in her first month at university, eighteen years old and with no experience of men, the word, anything. Suddenly she meets someone and wants to marry! In the space of three weeks, for heaven's sake! Obviously I thought it unreal. I continued to think it would die its natural death—I make no apology for that.'

Janine sighed, wanting to remain angry with him. But she did understand his initial reaction, she always had. Still ... 'I understand all that, Nikolai. But let's not forget the insults you came out with in Lille, the fact that you thought the marriage a mésalliance.'

'I meant it,' he said simply, looking her straight in the eyes. 'When I said it, I meant it. But I was wrong. I'm not so proud that I can't admit to making a mistake. I made a mistake in not getting to know Robert, and the family he belongs to. Your parents are fine people—you were right when you said Lara would be gaining by marrying into such a family. I've had a long talk with your parents. Your mother is warm and charming and your father is a very intelligent man. All that I'm saying to you, I've said to them.

'Mésalliance was too strong a word. Nevertheless I still have my doubts about this marriage. Lara has been spoilt, she's always had everything she's wanted. She's never had to do anything for herself. I wonder how she'll cope as the wife of a man who has a lot of work ahead of him in trying to get established, and I wonder how much they'll have in common when the honeymoon is over, what sort of foundation they have.'

'What sort of foundation?' Janine echoed. 'Love, Nikolai! They're *in love*. Really, I'm not sure what your recipe is for a successful marriage, but you certainly overlook this ingredient!'

'Ah, yes,' he smiled, 'this thing they call romantic love. I still don't know what it means, "in love", but whatever Lara feels for your brother must be very strong indeed for her to act against my wishes. That's something she's never done before. And you must remember, Janine, that I've been more like a father to her than a brother. Surely that will help you to understand my reaction last October? Your parents understood it very well.'

'I did—do—understand it.' She sighed inwardly, not wanting her hatred of him to diminish, but it was diminishing ... 'Why didn't you stay around after the wedding?'

'Because I didn't want to upset anyone with an unexpected appearance. Because it was only when I saw it with my own eyes, after three months had passed, that I believed the affair was more than an affair. Because I had to think all over again. It was a fait accompli. It was then, only then, that I considered all the things you had said to me. That there was nothing to be gained by my refusing to see Lara again, that she might need me at some point in the future, if things go wrong, but would be too proud to come to me. I knew you were right about that. The girl has a fierce sense of pride.'

'Yes, she has. No doubt my father's told you she's never mentioned your name in all these weeks. But she'll be delighted to see you on Saturday.' Janine felt suddenly drained, tired. 'Let's go and eat. We're parked illegally here.'

Just then her parents drove past them. They tooted

and waved but didn't stop to ask whether anything was wrong.

Nikolai didn't make a move. 'Have we cleared the air? Do you still find me despicable?'

Almost reluctantly, she said, 'We've cleared the air.' He was looking at her expectantly, waiting for an answer to his second question. 'I—when someone readily admits to making a mistake, it's hard to go on resenting them for that mistake.' She was hesitant to add more but his silence, his look, obliged her to. 'You—your explanations have made you more tolerable.'

Janine was not prepared to be more generous than that. She felt that she and Nikolai had reached a plateau; she wanted them to stay there for the time being. Or was it that she was afraid to move on and discover more, because she might stop hating him at all if she did that?

However, she had no choice in the matter. Nikolai was determined to set things straight between them. 'More tolerable? Is that all?'

'Can we drive on, please? I'm hungry.'

'No. We're not going anywhere until this conversation is finished. Once I start this car, I don't want to hear another word about your brother and my sister. So let's have it. What else is bothering you?'

'Nothing.'

'Then you'll admit that I'm not the bastard you took me for?'

'I'll admit that you're entitled to your point of view,' Janine said quietly, responding to his persistence. 'But I don't have to like it. I think you're an inveterate snob, and I haven't forgotten your treatment of me in Lille.'

'Ah! The servants' quarters . . .' He laughed, amused by the memory. 'Tempers were flaring that night, Janine. Yours as well as mine. Remember that. Come on now,' he coaxed, 'I've admitted mésalliance was the wrong word—and that's what started our fight.'

'So you're apologising for your treatment of me?'

'No,' he said simply, shrugging. 'You flung some pretty harsh insults yourself, but I'll admit I did nothing to put you right. In fact I acted according to what you thought of me. But you don't know what I'm really like, do you? So like I said, let's start afresh, shall we? Let's get to know each other properly.'

What could she say? Strangely, perversely, she respected him for not apologising. She would rather that than have him saying something he didn't mean. Piece by piece he had removed the ammunition she had held in store for a fight with him. In fact, they had not fought at all, they had had a discussion. There was, really, nothing left for her to be angry about. Her hatred of him had been neutralised with every passing minute.

'I—yes. All right, we'll start afresh.' What else could she have said? Anything else would have sounded peevish, unreasonable.

'Why so hesitant?' he asked. 'What are you thinking now?'

It was a good question, and she didn't really know the answer to it. All sorts of thoughts were going through her mind, confusing thoughts. If she had not felt so confused at that moment she might have said something constructive. As it was she shrugged helplessly. 'Why should it matter to you what I'm thinking?'

'Because I want this week to be pleasant. I don't want you to entertain me under sufferance.'

'Sufferance? No,' she said slowly, thoughtful, 'it won't be that. Not now. I—I understand you much better now.'

She turned away as he started the engine, looking out of the window but not seeing anything. On route to the hotel nothing else was said, apart from her giving him directions.

From time to time she glanced at him as the confusion in her mind disappeared and several things became startlingly clear to her. In the middle of their conversation she had told herself she didn't want to discover anything else about Nikolai, but she had discovered things about him. In talking about someone else, she had learned things about Nikolai with every sentence he spoke. There were several things she had to admire: his honesty in saying what he thought, his admission that he had been wrong in not getting to know Robbie, the fact that he was here, now, to put things right.

And she respected him for all this, for the fact that he was true to himself, and by no means too arrogant or too proud to bury the hatchet. Her original opinion of Nikolai had been wrong, quite wrong, she was forced to admit that now. During the past half hour she had had just a glimpse of what he was really like, and she was pleased by what she had seen.

CHAPTER SEVEN

'YOU'RE very quiet, Janine.' Nikolai turned to her after ordering drinks from the waiter in the bar. 'I see there's a grill room and a restaurant here. Where would you prefer to eat?'

'In the restaurant.' She smiled at him. She hadn't realised how quiet she had been until he had pointed it out to her. 'Sorry if I seem subdued, I'm a bit tired. I've had a long day.'

'That's all right. And how was London?' The smile she had given him was rewarded by one of his own, and Janine felt herself relaxing as they fell into conversation and she chatted about Pauline Norris and their week-end.

When the waiter brought the menus, she asked Nikolai to order for her, excused herself and headed for the ladies' room. The bar was in an open area which led off in several directions and she was aware of Nikolai's eyes following her as she crossed the floor. What she needed was a few minutes away from him, time to take stock.

She looked at her reflection in the mirror, relieved to see that she didn't look as confused and bewildered as she felt. Actually, it was these things which had made her subdued, rather than tiredness.

Ever since her first meeting with Nikolai she had been obsessed with him, it had been as though she were the victim of some sort of emotional sabotage by him. And now—now she was being manipulated by circumstances, thrust into his company, and she no longer had her hatred of him to—to protect her.

Further confused by that thought, she stared at her reflection. Protect her? Protect her from what? And how could it be that suddenly she found herself looking forward to the week ahead? Looking forward to it, yet vaguely worried by the prospect . . .

What on earth was wrong with her? She absolutely must sort herself out! She combed her hair and freshened her lipstick, falling back on the common sense which always used to dictate her thoughts, her actions. She must resurrect that common sense now. There was really nothing at all to worry about; all she needed to do was to treat Nikolai according to what he was: her brother's brother-in-law. No more, no less.

As she walked back into the bar she saw that there were fresh drinks on the table. Nikolai was still reading the menu, oblivious to the interested gaze he was getting from an attractive brunette sitting a few yards away.

Janine was in the centre of the room when a pair of strong arms suddenly closed around her from behind. She squealed in surprise, aware of heads turning in her direction.

Michael Granger stepped in front of her, his arms sliding possessively around her waist. 'Hello, my lovely!' He kissed her briefly on the lips. 'What are you doing here, and where are we going later on?'

'Oh, Michael, you gave me a fright!' She looked up at him, laughing. 'I'm having dinner here, of course. And you?'

'The same. Call it a duty dinner. I'm with my father. Mum's on the mainland till Wednesday, so I called round to see him and coaxed him out. He's in the restaurant. Actually, we've almost finished, so I'll be free in an hour or so when when I've taken him home.' He glanced around the bar, frowning because there was no one around whom he recognised. 'Who are you with?'

Janine nodded in the direction of Nikolai, whose eyes had been on them since she was intercepted. 'Lara's brother. Would you believe it?'

At first Michael looked pleased, his eyebrows going up in surprise. He had been told by Janine only the vaguest details of her initial meeting with Nikolai. All he had really needed to know was the reason the wedding had had to be held in France, so she had told him very little else—except what she had thought of Nikolai as a person.

Then he looked vaguely disgruntled, glancing at her quickly as he sized the other man up. 'He's a handsome b——I mean, he's a handsome devil, isn't he?'

'Devil being the operative word,' Janine said dismissively. She was not about to tell Michael that she had changed her opinion of Nikolai. 'I won't bother introducing you.'

'No, do introduce me,' Michael said slowly, looking a little puzzled now. 'He looks familiar. I'm sure I've seen him somewhere before.'

Janine did not want this. Why, she couldn't be sure, nor was she sure of the reason she didn't want to tell Michael she had misjudged Nikolai. 'But your father——'

'Is on his third brandy and perfectly happy. He'll realise I've bumped into someone I know.'

That was true enough. Michael was well known on the island, in the context of lifelong resident, playboy and businessman. He linked her arm through his own and walked towards Nikolai.

The Frenchman stood up, giving a brief but deferential bow of his head to Janine.

She kept the introductions brief and formal. 'Nikolai, I'd like you to meet Michael Granger. Michael is an old friend of mine and of Robert. He was best man at your sister's wedding.' She turned to Michael, whose arm was now around her waist again. 'Michael, this is Count Nikolai Andreivitch Nekrassov, Lara's brother. He's staying with us for a few days until she comes home from her honeymoon on Saturday.'

She was watching Michael's eyes, waiting for signs of surprise as Nikolai's full title registereed with him. He had had no idea that Lara was a Countess; Lara did not go around telling people, and she certainly didn't look like a Countess in her regular uniform of jeans and a jumper . . . unlike her brother, whose very presence in a room commanded attention.

Michael was surprised, but not for the reasons she expected. His arm dropped from her waist as he reached out to shake hands with Nikolai. 'Nekrassov,' he said, looking astonished and pleased. 'Sabre Cars. Of *course*, Sabre Cars!' He spoke to Janine in a tone which was almost accusing. 'Why didn't you tell me who Lara's brother is? I mean, I heard her maiden name, knew it was familiar but promptly forgot it!' He was shaking Nikoai's hand vigorously.

Without a word, Nikolai sat down.

The others followed suit and Michael leaned towards the Frenchman as if he were waiting to be recognised. 'We've met before, Nikolai. A year ago, at a big charity do in London. At the Savoy, remember? I was with my mother, who sits on umpteen committees all over the show. You give a great deal to charity, I believe. Or rather your firm does. Well, it's the same thing. Do you know, I've been waiting eighteen months to take delivery of one of your cars? That's six months more than I expected to wait.'

Janine was loooking from one man to the next, nonplussed. Nikolai had said not a word in confirmation or denial of anything Michael had said. Not that Michael had given him a chance. But Michael had finished now—and Nikolai was merely smiling.

She had the distinct feeling that the deep blue eyes had taken Michael apart, examined him and put him back together again in the space of two or three minutes. She would be interested to know what Nikolai's findings were. But she would never ask. Obliged to fill in the sudden silence, she said, 'I had no idea, Michael. You never told me you'd ordered a new car.'

He smiled, all his fondness and affection for her plain

to see. 'Ah, but you don't know about everything that happens in my life, my darling.' He took her hand and raised it to his lips. 'Alas and alas and alas.' And with that, he kissed her hand again, lingeringly.'

Her eyes met those of Nikolai and she saw his mind filing away this new information. One eyebrow rose sardonically and the smile on his lips was faint now, faint and taunting.

'I'm afraid you were misinformed.' he said at last, addressing Michael. 'Eighteen months is the usual waiting time for a specialist car such as Sabre.'

Michael shrugged goodnaturedly. 'Shipping thousands of 'em over to Saudi every year, eh? Business must be good.'

'We don't make thousands every year,' Nikolai corrected, his voice uninterested. 'Do you want to hang on a little longer or do you want to cancel? You can give me the details now, if you're sick of waiting.'

Michael seemed to think he was joking. He threw back his head and laughed. 'Not likely! Here, I tell you what though ...' He took a business card from his pocket and handed it over. 'Give me a ring when you get back to France, would you? Let me know the state of play.'

Nikolai pocketed the card without comment, without looking at it.

'Look, I won't stay for a drink,' Michael went on. 'But why don't we all get together later? Bring Nikolai down to Bunny's,' he said to Janine. 'Some of the gang will be there.'

'Bunny's is a disco,' Janine explained. 'One of Michael's regular haunts.'

'That's very kind of you,' Nikolai said to Michael, 'but we won't join you. Janine and I have a great deal to talk about.'

This was said with such authority that Michael was left with no answer, nor was he aware that he had not, in fact, been invited to have a drink with them now. He seemed unaware of Nikolai's lack of interest in him and anything he had to say. He got to his feet. 'Then join us on Friday, will you? Perhaps parties are your scene?'

Janine glanced from one man to the next, suppressing laughter at the look on Nikolai's face.

'Us?' he queried, looking from her to Michael. 'Are you suggesting a threesome? Janine has a date on Friday—with you, presumably. And you want me to join you?'

He was deliberately misunderstanding, Janine knew, and Michael was laughing his head off. 'Jan, you never told me Nikolai has such a dry sense of humour! No, old chap, I'm definitely not suggesting a threesome!' He was laughing like a drain, and careless because of it. 'I spend half my life trying to get Janine out alone, but there's no chance of that on Friday. You wouldn't be playing gooseberry, if that's what you're worried about!'

Janine groaned inwardly. Michael was saying far more than she wanted Nikolai to know, and Nikolai did not look worried about anything. He just continued coolly to survey Michael, waiting for an explanation.

'My family is giving a party.' Michael sobered at last, brushing away a lock of fair hair which had fallen over his forehead. 'At my parents' house. It'll be quite a do. It's to celebrate our having been in business for a quarter of a century. Anyhow, you're welcome to come along. I'll be glad to see you.'

'Thank you.'

'I'd better go. See you Friday.' With that, Michael stooped to kiss Janine's cheek, giving her a reassuring squeeze on the shoulder as he did so.

She smiled as he walked away. He was such a nice person. She might have known he would ask Nikolai to the party on Friday; he'd done it for her sake, of course. He would never dream that Nikolai was any kind of threat. Why should he, when he thought she still hated the man? He was probably inwardly sympathising with her because it was her duty to entertain this—house guest.

She picked up her aperitif, her second, and glanced at Nikolai over the rim of the glass. He was studying the wine list now, and Janine studied him, intrigued by the clever way he had handled Michael, dismissing him but doing so without any hint of rudeness.

They were halfway through their hors d'oeuvres when Nikolai took the business card from his pocket. 'Jewellery,' he said, and Janine watched with mild surprise as he tore the card into neat, small pieces and dropped it in the ashtray. 'So you've got yourself a Jersey millionaire, by the look of things.'

'What—I'm not sure what you mean.'

'I mean, are you in some way committed to Granger?'

'No,' she said quietly. She had wanted to tell him that this was none of his business, but somehow the answer didn't come out like that.

'He wants you.'

'Yes.'

'You like him very much.'

'Yes, and I'm very fond of him. We've been friends for a long time.'

'But you have never been lovers.' It was a statement, not a question, and this time she said nothing. This really was none of his business.

The Frenchman did not repeat himself. He didn't need to, he just smiled. 'I take it he's asked you to marry him?'

Janine shrugged. This was no secret. 'Several times.'

'So why don't you?'

She blinked at that. 'Do you really need to ask?'

'Of course I need to ask. He may not be your lover, but you certainly don't find him unattractive. Granger is a handsome man with a great deal going for him . . . How old is he?'

'Thirty.'

'And you? Twenty-five? Twenty-four?'

'Twenty-three.'

He nodded briefly. 'A beautiful, sophisticated young woman who obviously has some experience of the world. But you're not a dedicated career girl, you're ripe for marriage now. So tell me, why haven't you accepted Granger's offer?'

Janine leaned back in her chair, bemused. 'Because,'

she said slowly, clearly, watching his eyes, 'I'm not in love with him.'

Nikolai laughed at that. 'There you go again! I've told you before, you're an unrealistic romantic. You know my views on that—in love. What does it mean?'

Fortunately he didn't really expect her to answer, because she would have had difficulty in defining something she had not experienced but which she believed in. One thing was for certain: while Lara had exaggerated many aspects of Nikolai's personality, negative aspects, she had been absolutely right in saying he'd never been in love. And she was no doubt right in saying he was incapable of falling in love, too, since he had reached the age of thirty-five and he was openly sceptical of the concept. This, despite the many women he had known.

Janine watched him as he picked up his wineglass and drank deeply, thoughtful, and wondered what was going through his mind now.

'What sort of car is Granger driving at the moment?'

She started laughing. Of all the things, questions, which might have been going through his mind, this was least expected! 'A Rolls Corniche.'

'Shame,' he said drily. 'He'll just have to manage with that till he gets his Sabre.'

This struck Janine as hilarious, not only Nikolai's wit but also the fact that he had been irritated by Michael over the car business. She hadn't realised it before. 'Oh, the Sabre won't be a replacement,' she said impishly. 'Knowing Michael, he'll use it as a spare once the novelty has worn off.'

Nikolai rose to it. 'So he isn't an enthusiast,' he said, with a certain amount of distaste. 'He's one of those people who treats cars as if they were toys.'

Janine laughed heartily, so much so that people turned to look at her. And the more she tried to control it, the less able she was. Then Nikolai was laughing, too, not because he understood her laughter but because he was enjoying the sight of her. 'Are you winding me around, you little witch?'

This set her off even further and as much as she was

feeling selfconscious, she couldn't stop laughing. 'Up,' she almost choked. 'The expression is, are you winding me *up*?'

'Whatever!' He was laughing at himself now, and that was very much a point in his favour as far as Janine was concerned.

'Ah! So you can laugh at yourself as well as admit your mistakes!' she giggled. 'Perhaps you're not so bad after all.'

'Such compliments!' He saluted her with his wine glass as the waiter came to clear their plates. 'And you were winding me up, weren't you?'

'Yes and no. I have no idea what Michael's plans are as far as his new car's concerned!'

Nikolai handed the ashtray to the waiter, his grin a sudden flash of white against the tan of his skin. He was getting rid of Michael's business card, and Janine laughed at the symbolism. 'Now tell me about yourself,' he said.

'Ask away. Be specific, unless you want the story of my life!'

'Ah, but I do, Janine, I do . . .'

That was all it took. Whether it was her consumption of wine after two aperitifs which made her so relaxed, she didn't stop to wonder. Or perhaps it was their shared laughter that did it. Whatever the cause, the effect was the removal of barriers, defences, and she found herself talking to him easily, unselfconsciously.

The evening sped by very pleasantly, and neither of them noticed how long they had lingered, how quickly the hours had passed. It was only when Janine glanced around the restaurant that she realised how late it was. 'Heavens, we're almost the last people in here, and we came so early!'

'Does it matter?'

There was something about his tone which brought her eyes right back to his. 'No. No, not at all.'

'How about a final cup of coffee and a cognac?'

'Why not?'

He signalled the waiter, turning to Janine with a

roguish glint in his eyes. 'You didn't really think me the type who'd enjoy a disco, did you?'

'No,' she grinned. 'To tell the truth, I don't particularly like them myself. But the crowd there are a lot of fun and it's . . . something to do.'

He considered this, his expression serious, but made no comment. 'This, to me, is the perfect evening—a leisurely dinner with a beautiful woman, good conversation, good wine. I've enjoyed it very much, Janine. Thank you.'

'Thank you,' she amended.

There was a sudden silence. It was not an awkward silence but a companionable one. They both went into their own thoughts, not feeling the need to talk. The waiter placed her cognac and coffee before her and Janine idly fingered the spoon, silently agreeing that this was her idea of a perfect evening, too . . . a leisurely dinner with a handsome man, good conversation, good wine . . . but she was surprised to find herself feeling this way when Nikolai Nekrassov was the man concerned, very surprised.

Almost unwillingly her eyes moved to his face. He was lighting a cheroot, the flame from his lighter casting a fleeting shadow over the lean, sculptured features.

It struck her suddenly, unexpectedly, a swift snap of desire for him which shot through her entire body, making her tingle down to her fingertips, invoking memories . . . 'I—er—I thought we'd head east tomorrow, Nikolai. We can have lunch in Gorey and I'll show you Mont Orgueil Castle. It's a must for tourists.'

'Tourists?' The word made him smile. He shrugged, bowing his head as the blue of his eyes lit with amusement. 'As you say, *mademoiselle*. I am in your hands, *n'est-ce-pas?*'

'You—you are a guest of my family,' she answered, refusing to acknowledge any ambiguity in what he had said, unsure whether in fact there had been any.

Tuesday was glorious. It was the second week of March

and the weather was being exceptionally kind. Janine shivered against the warmth of the sun as they emerged from the dank coldness of the German Underground Hospital, a left-over from the war years, in St Lawrence.

Nikolai had wanted to see the place. He had had his own ideas, so they had headed west instead of east!

'Well?' she said.

'Fascinating.' He took her arm as they talked. 'Depressing, interesting, it made me think of——'

'I didn't mean the hospital!' She laughed a little too loudly, acutely conscious of the feel of his hand on her arm. 'I meant what now? Is there anything else you particularly want to see or am I in charge now?'

'*Ma chère* Janine! Of course you are in charge. I told you last night, I am in your hands . . .'

Fortunately he had not been in her hands the previous night. Or rather, she had not been in his. Her mother and father were at home when they got back from the hotel, at home and drinking coffee, waiting for them. Janine had never been quite so relieved to see them, grateful for their thoughtfulness in coming home early and skipping their post-Bridge socialising. No doubt they had had a twinge of conscience at the way they'd thrown Janine in at the deep end.

But she was no longer in at the deep end. She was enjoying herself and she wasn't afraid to admit it. 'What does this mean?' She looked at the keys Nikolai dropped into her hand.

'It means you do the driving from now on—just to prove you're in charge of this tour.'

'Oh, I don't think——'

'Come on.' He opened the car door for her and ushered her in. 'What are you so nervous about?' he asked, as he settled in the passenger seat.

Janine looked dubiously at the dashboard. 'Driving on the left with a left-hand drive, for one thing! All those horses under the bonnet for another. What you'll say to me if I scratch the paintwork for another. And I'm not sure——'

'You disappoint me,' he interrupted. 'Have you a

faint heart, Janine? I would not have thought so. Now come on, just treat the accelerator with respect and she won't run away with you.'

'I'd better,' she muttered, 'there's a forty miles an hour speed limit on the island.'

'What?'

She didn't dare look at him. Her lower lip was caught between her teeth in an effort to prevent laughter bubbling out of her.

'Everywhere?' he demanded. 'Does that apply to the entire island?'

She nodded, still avoiding looking at him.

'Well, you might have told me earlier! You might have told me before you asked me to show you what the car was capable of!'

Her laughter gurgled against her closed mouth. 'I might.' And then it came in a torrent, and she was helpless. 'But we were on a clear stretch of road! And it was early morning. Why worry? We didn't get caught!'

'And that makes it all right?'

She ventured a look, hoping he wasn't really as cross as he sounded. 'But I like driving fast, Nikolai! And I wanted you to show me——'

He reached out to her, putting the palm of his hand against her cheek and looking at her as an expert might look at a beautiful painting. 'Beautiful,' he said slowly, his eyes, his expression intense. 'Your face, your skin, those green eyes moist with tears.'

Tears of laughter. They had gathered in her eyes and she was seeing him through a slight haze. But she sobered instantly at his touch, his words. Silent seconds slipped by and questions were being asked again by both pairs of eyes.

From close by a car horn tooted and the moment was shattered. Startled, Janine looked around, irritated by the culprit who had spoiled the moment, yet grateful at the same time.

'You'd better move the car,' Nikolai said quietly, glancing in the direction of the man who had tooted. 'We're blocking him in.'

She fumbled with the ignition, her hands trembling,

and Nikolai looked at her worriedly. 'Hey, take it easy. You'll do just fine. It's only a heap of metal, when all's said and done!'

She smiled and slipped the gear lever smoothly into reverse, knowing a sudden rush of gratitude towards him. It was sweet of him to reassure her like that, but he had misunderstood why her hands were trembling.

Last night, in bed, in the silence of her room she had reviewed with nothing less than amazement the hours she had spent with Nikolai. What a day yesterday had been, from leaving Pauline Norris in London in the afternoon to the shock, which had not been a shock, of finding Nikolai in her home. From shouting abuse at him to a heated discussion with him ... to a perfect evening with him.

She had been thrust on to a journey of discovery but she was no longer an unwilling passenger. She glanced at him, now, as she drove the powerful Sabre along the winding lanes of the island, pleased, flattered, to see that he was so relaxed with her at the wheel of his car. It gave her confidence.

'Pull up a moment,' he said then.

She did as he asked and he reached for a button on the dashboard. Janine heard a click followed by a gentle humming noise, and the roof of the car slid slowly backwards. As she drove on again the warm wind lifted her hair and she revelled in the feeling of freedom, revelled in the glory of the day. The sky was a perfect azure, cloudless, and the sun, not yet at its meridian, was warm against her skin, giving her a sense of well-being.

Like tourists, they took photographs when they got to Mont Orgueil Castle. Like tourists they explored the nearby harbour, Janine enjoying herself as though she were seeing these sights for the first time. They discussed the history of the island, with which Nikolai was familiar, from the days when Jersey had been part of the Duchy of Normandy, to the attacks it had been subjected to by France during the fourteenth and fifteenth centuries, to its occupation by German forces in the 'forties.

For lunch they went to a little bistro Janine frequented regularly because the food was good and the prices reasonable, and before they had finished eating they were making plans for the following day. Having mentioned that she liked riding and did it regularly, Nikolai suggested that that was what they would do the following afternoon.

'You've remembered that I'm going shopping in the morning?'

'I've remembered. And I'm having a round of golf with your father.'

She looked up in surprise, spooning the last of the cream from her dish of strawberries. 'Really? I shouldn't have thought you were the type.'

'I'm not the type. I haven't played for several years. I warned Archie about that!'

'And when was all this arranged?' she asked.

'This morning, at breakfast, before you put in an appearance.' He grinned as he sat back, stretching, unaware of what the slow, lazy movement did to Janine's imagination. At least she hoped he was unaware. The sleeves of his sweater were pushed back on his forearms and she could see the dark hair against the tan of his skin, could see the movement of muscle and tendons as he flexed his arms.

'Janine?'

It was only as he spoke her name that she realised she'd been staring at him. She shrugged nonchalantly. 'I was just thinking that if I hadn't met you before, that is if I didn't know otherwise, I would never have suspected you had a foul and violent temper.'

'I could say the same thing about you,' he pointed out, smiling.

Janine thought about that when she was lying in bed that night. By rights she should have fallen asleep at once because the day had been a long one and quite tiring. Instead she found herself thinking about the man in the bedroom just two doors away from her own.

Certainly she had seen the worst side of him in Lille—but then he had seen the worst side of her, too, especially during breakfast on the morning she left, when she had been extremely sarcastic.

She wondered what he thought of her now, then she told herself it didn't really matter. But somehow she couldn't quite convince herself of that, and with a conscious effort she switched her thoughts to the shopping trip she and her mother were taking in the morning, determined that if something had to keep her from sleeping, it must not be thoughts of Nikolai that did it.

CHAPTER EIGHT

ON Thursday they went sightseeing again, winding their way from west to east along the north coast of the island. Janine did the driving so Nikolai could take in the scenery, though it started to rain heavily during mid-afternoon. They stopped for tea in a café in Bouley Bay and ordered scones with strawberry jam and Jersey cream.

Time was passing too quickly, and they had crammed so much into the past few days. Last night they had played a far from serious game of Scrabble with Archie and Rose, and yesterday afternoon they had been riding and playing tennis. During the early evening they had walked on the beach, and Nikolai had had Janine in stitches, relating some incidents from the travelling he had done when he left university, before settling down to work in the factory.

'More tea?'

Nikolai leaned towards her, his tone confidential. 'Do you know that until today I haven't drunk tea for—oh, three or four years?'

'Is that a fact?' she said dramatically, shaking her head in mock disgust. 'Well, you could hardly drink coffee at a traditional moment like this, not with scones and jam! I mean to say, it would hardly be right, would it?' she giggled.

He leaned closer, twining his fingers into the dark blonde curls of her hair, his indigo eyes smiling at her. 'If you say so, beautiful lady.'

Janine reached for the teapot, pulling away from him because his nearness was too disturbing. She handed him his cup, only to find that his eyes were laughing at her now. He knew, he *knew* the effect he had on her.

It was still pouring with rain when they left the café and they ran for the car, laughing as it turned into a race—which Nikolai won.

'Hey, you're out of condition!' His accusation came as they got into the car, and Janine protested strongly.

'I am not! It's just that you've got longer legs!' She poked him playfully in the ribs. 'I'm as fit as——'

It happened then. In one easy movement he reached for her, pulling her tightly against him as he cut off her words with a kiss.

Janine struggled for freedom, horrified by her body's reactions, by the immediate rush of desire she felt for him. She had known how she would feel if he kissed her. It was still there, the powerful, compelling, physical attraction which had been born in Lille the first time they had touched, triggered simply by his fingers accidentally brushing against hers.

And now he was kissing her as ardently as he had kissed her in her bedroom later that night, when they had both taken time to savour first the pleasure of each other's lips. But she did not want to make that discovery all over again, not now, not when she felt so much more vulnerable because she had grown to like him . . .

She pulled away from him, her eyes bright with panic at the way she was feeling. 'Nikolai, please——'

'Please what? What, Janine?' The deep blue eyes were all-knowing as he caught her face between his hands, forcing her to look at him.

But she couldn't answer him, she couldn't move, she could hardly breathe for the way her heart was throbbing crazily inside her.

Nikolai nodded slowly, knowing precisely how she

was feeling. 'Yes, it's still there. Did you think it would have faded with the passing of a few months?'

He got his answer by kissing her again, but differently this time. Very slowly, very lightly, his lips brushed against hers with intoxicating sweetness. And this time, curiously, it was the very absence of passion which excited her, the very gentleness of his kiss which prevented her from resisting. Maybe it was because she felt safer, more able to cope when he kissed her this way ... or maybe it was because she knew the passion was there all the time, merely being held in check ...

His lips trailed down to her neck, moving lightly against the soft skin as his hands moved over the firm swell of her breasts, barely touching but teasing their responsive nipples as they hardened against the light brush of his palms. 'We have unfinished business, haven't we, Janine? And before this week is out, we're going to be lovers.'

'No!' She stilled his hands, trying to move away from him, but his arms slid around her waist and held her tightly.

'Don't say no when you mean yes. We both know what happened to us that night in Lille,' he murmured against her neck. 'It won't be denied, Janine. It's there constantly, every time we touch.'

Desire. It was there constantly, she couldn't deny it. But she had no intention of giving in to it, no matter how compelling. She thrust herself away from him. 'I think we'd better go home,' she said stiffly. 'I—my mother will get anxious if we're not back in good time to go out tonight.'

Nikolai was taking them all out to dinner tonight. He had invited her parents out over breakfast that morning, easily sweeping aside her mother's protests that she loved cooking for people. He had said he wanted to reciprocate her parents' hospitality and that Rose must allow him to do so. Of course Rose was delighted; she had remarked more than once to her daughter that she thought Nikolai a charming man.

He was watching her closely now. 'What's the problem?'

'What? I—nothing.' She opened the car door rather shakily. 'I'll take the passenger seat, Nikolai. I never did like driving in a downpour.'

They swapped seats, and she turned her attention to the passing scenery as they drove home, feeling acutely disturbed by his nearness, as if suddenly she were in danger . . .

Janine laid the black dress on her bed and slipped her housecoat on over her underwear. It was Friday, the night of Michael's party, and she had bathed and done her make-up, but she still had her hair to do. It took her longer than it should have, maybe because she was feeling depressed at the knowledge that this week was nearly over.

While they were out to dinner with her parents the previous evening, Nikolai had said he would sail back to France on Sunday, that he had a business meeting on Monday morning. Tomorrow evening, Saturday, would of course be spent with Lara and Robbie, and Janine was going with Nikolai to meet them at the airport in the afternoon.

'Need any help, Jan? Time's getting on, it's almost nine o'clock.' Rose came into the room and sat on the edge of the bed, eyeing the dress she had helped her daughter to choose.

'I'm managing, thanks.' Janine was putting the finished touches to her hair. 'It doesn't matter about the time. The party will only just be getting under way. Needless to say we'll be home very late tonight.'

'Well, I've no intention of waiting up for you, darling!' laughed Rose, still looking thoughtfully at the dress. 'You know what sort of effect this will have on Michael!'

Janine had had no doubts about the dress when they had chosen it, but she was having misgivings now. It was black, with thin shoulder-straps, it was full length and made from a silky, fairly heavy material. The neckline was as low as the backline, a simple V, and the dress fitted her perfectly, clinging to the contours of her body. And yes, she knew what it would do to Michael.

But it wasn't the effect on Michael Granger she was worried about now . . .

She glanced at her mother via the dressing table mirror. 'Michael is no problem to me, Mum. I've been keeping him in line for years. Besides, I'll be chaperoned by Nikolai, and Michael will be circulating among his guests for most of the evening.'

This provoked more laughter from Rose. 'But you don't think Nikolai will be immune to the way this looks on you?'

'I have no idea,' Janine said coolly, shifting a little so she could avoid her mother's curious gaze.

'Nikolai's turned out to be not in the least what we expected, hasn't he? And handsome? *Mon Dieu*, he's good-looking!'

'Yes.' There was no denying that, any of it.

'And what about Michael?' her mother probed. 'You've been seeing a lot more of him these past few months. I know how he feels about you—everyone knows how he feels about you!—but how do you feel these days?'

'The same,' Janine said airily.

Rose shrugged philosophically. 'I'll see you downstairs, darling.'

Janine surveyed herself critically in the full-length mirror before going downstairs, wishing then that her mother had stayed to give her reassurance about the dress, or rather the neckline of it. Surely it was a little too . . . *too!*

But in the shop her mother had said she thought it perfect for Janine, and Rose had superb dress sense; her opinion could be relied upon. Besides, it was too late now, there was nothing else in her wardrobe which was sufficiently dressy for tonight.

Nikolai and her parents were having a drink when she went down and joined them. He had on the light grey suit he had worn on their first evening, this time with a blue shirt which almost matched the colour of his eyes. Those eyes went straight to Janine as she entered the room and he smiled slowly, approvingly, as he took in the sight of her.

Archie and Rose fussed admiringly over her dress, her appearance. She had swept her hair up into a chignon, leaving wispy curls around the hairline to add softness to the style. At her throat she wore a slim gold necklace which Michael had given her, and the earrings to match.

Nikolai said nothing. He just looked.

It was only when they got into his car that he said something about her appearance. He switched on the engine and left it ticking over while his eyes swept slowly over her from the tip of her high-heeled shoes to the top of her head. 'Very sophisticated and very, very chic,' he said in French, his voice serious and quiet. And with that he leaned close to her and let his lips brush lightly over the pulse points of her neck. 'And you're wearing Dior again . . . *Ma chère* Janine, you are a walking aphrodisiac . . .'

The party was well under way, the house ablaze with lights and humming with music which for the moment was of the background variety, unobtrusive. It was a very big house, expensively and tastefully furnished. In the meticulously groomed gardens there was a swimming pool, and lanterns had been hung outside for the occasion. A few people were on the patio, drinking, for the evening was mild and a full moon was shining from a clear black sky studded with stars.

There was a bar on the patio as well as one indoors, and it was there that Michael came hurrying to greet the newcomers, apologising for having missed them at the door. But Janine and Nikolai had been descended upon instantly at the door by Gloria Warwick and her boy-friend, and then by Suzie Smythe—one of Michael's biggest fans.

Michael shook hands with Nikolai and then took hold of both Janine's hands, looking her over delightedly. 'Wow! You look stunning, darling! Absolutely, perfectly beautiful!'

Aware of the smile Nikolai was no doubt suppressing, Michael's over-enthusiasm embarrassed her. 'Thank you,' she said lightly. 'You're looking pretty good yourself.'

'I'm never at home in a monkey suit,' he said as he kissed her cheek, 'but if it turns you on, I'll wear one daily!'

He gave Nikolai a man-to-man grin, which embarrassed Janine further, then slapped him heartily on the back. 'Glad you could make it, old man. I wasn't sure whether you'd have stayed around. Your sister gets home tomorrow, doesn't she?'

They ordered drinks from the bartender, one of the catering staff who had been hired for the evening, and Michael stayed with them for ten minutes or so before moving on to greet other new arrivals.

No sooner had he disappeared than Nikolai said, 'I'm beginning to have my doubts.'

'About what?' It was Janine who was suppressing a smile now, because Nikolai's eyes were glinting roguishly and she knew he was going to be sarcastic about Michael.

'You and Granger. Your compatibility. He's too— ach! *Mon Dieu*, he's so—*English!*'

Janine was biting her cheeks, thinking that effusive would be a better description. 'But he isn't English,' she teased. 'Channel Islanders don't regard themselves as English.'

'I think you know very well what I was trying to say,' he retorted, his smile a sudden flash of white as she burst out laughing.

They went back indoors to an atmosphere which was full of chatter and laughter. The buffet tables were piled with food and the spread was magnificent. There was everything from the daintiest appetiser to cold roast chickens, sides of beef and pork, smoked salmon, game, a myriad salads to choose from and the most sinful, delicious-looking sweet dishes.

Janine knew a lot of the people present and she watched with a certain fascination the interest people showed when introduced to Nikolai, most especially the women. Young and old alike, married, single or somewhere between, they eyed him speculatively. Some, naturally, were far more subtle about it than others, but it was interesting to see how Nikolai handled them.

And that was, Janine thought, exactly the right word for it.

There was no way he could have reached the age of thirty-five without being well aware of his attractiveness. Maybe it was his height, or the immaculate cut of his clothes, the way he wore them, or perhaps it was his air of self-possession, of confidence, which made him stand out in a crowd, which gave him what could only be described as presence. But there was nothing in his manner which gave the impression that he *was* aware of his handsomeness, his attributes—which in itself was attractive.

There were quite a few foreigners at the party, including a handful of French, and Nikolai seemed to have a knack of getting all kinds of people to talk to him, while he himself did very little talking. It made her feel flattered in thinking about the ease with which he talked to her when they were alone, because here he held much of his personality back, kept much of himself in reserve, yet he was charming and totally relaxed.

Perhaps it was this, this combination that created about him an air of mystery, which aroused the interest of the women. That, and his obvious physical attractiveness. He did not flirt, he never came close to it. Indeed Janine though it was not in his nature to flirt—he didn't need to! And she was not by his side all the time. More than once they were split up, chatting to different people, but she watched him constantly, very surreptitiously, fascinated by the different side to him she was seeing tonight, now they were among a crowd.

It was almost midnight when they helped themselves to some food, Janine piling her plate high while Nikolai leaned over and whispered in her ear. 'Let's eat and then run, okay?'

She laughed softly, tickled by his choice of words. 'Aren't you enjoying yourself?'

Deliberately he looked around, smiling falsely and nodding to everyone and no one in particular, speaking quietly so nobody could hear, while keeping the silly smile on his face. Janine was laughing her head off at him even before he spoke. 'I'm bored rigid!'

Her laughter faded, her eyes narrowing thoughtfully. 'I *wondered* about that ... Do you know, I thought as much? But you've made a damn good job of hiding it.' She said it with genuine admiration.

'Practice,' he shrugged. 'In my time, I've had plenty of it.'

She nodded slowly. 'A little world-weary, aren't you, Nikolai?'

And then he was serious, very. 'More than a little.'

'Well—please, let's hang on a bit longer. Michael's father is giving a speech at midnight, about the reason for the party, and it would be too rude to——'

'Of course.' Nikolai put some food on his plate, perfectly agreeable, just as Michael appeared and asked to 'borrow' Janine for a while.

'Darling, it's one minute to midnight, and Dad wants me to give the speech, you know, to thank everyone for coming and so on. He says he hasn't got the wind for it. Come with me, come and stand by me.'

He whisked Janine away, shouting above the crowd until he had everyone's attention. The music was turned off while he spoke to his guests, who responded with things like, 'And here's to the next twenty-five years!' 'Here's to the next million, Michael!'

Then the music resumed at a much louder volume and the mood of the party changed completely, really going into full swing. People started dancing, inside, outside, everywhere. Michael took Janine into his arms, pleased and a little relieved at the way things had gone so far. 'It's a roaring success, eh, Jan?'

'It was bound to be.' She smiled, following his lead as they danced. 'You organised it.'

'I'll be glad when Nekrassov's left the island,' he said, suddenly changing the subject. 'I resent him!'

Janine blinked in surprise. 'What's brought that on?'

Michael pulled her closer, too close for her liking. 'Seeing you with him tonight. I thought you hated his guts?'

'I—well, I——'

'That's all changed,' he said flatly. 'Obviously. Every time I've looked at the pair of you you've been gazing at each other or laughing, sharing some little joke.'

'Oh, Michael, you're imagining things,' she laughed. 'You're exaggerating!'

He pulled back slightly so he could look at her directly. 'Just watch yourself with him, Jan.'

Patiently she said, 'Now what's that supposed to mean?'

'I don't have to draw pictures for you. He's far more experienced than you, he fancies himself and he's— slick, too bloody slick!'

Tongue in cheek she thanked him for the warning, even though he'd been unfair. Nikolai could not be accused of fancying himself, far from it. She excused herself from Michael and went upstairs to one of the bathrooms, regretting that she hadn't had a chance to finish her food. After several glasses of champagne, she felt she needed it.

Gloria Warwick stepped out of the bathroom just as Janine reached the door. 'Well, you're a fine one!' she said accusingly. 'You've had this dish of a man staying with you all week and you've kept him to yourself! Not that I blame you, mind. No wonder we haven't seen you lately!'

By that she meant the crowd, the clique Michael moved in. 'Hello, Gloria.' Janine said it nicely, but she was not about to launch into an explanation she didn't owe anyone. In any case, Suzie Smythe appeared before she had a chance to say anything else.

'Hi, Gloria, Jan. Who *is* that man you're with?'

'Oh, he's only the owner of Sabre Cars, if you don't mind!' Gloria giggled, looking curiously at Janine. 'I've been asking Michael about him. It seems he made a pile of money from patenting some of his mechanical gadgets—quite apart from what his factory makes.'

'He's my brother's brother-in-law,' Janine said casually, giving Suzie the information she had really been after.

Gloria excused herself, and Suzie (who was actually in love with Michael, though no one was supposed to know it) went on, 'I saw you both strolling along the beach this morning. You didn't see me. I'd have come to you for an introduction if I'd been looking my best—which I wasn't!'

Janine just smiled. 'Well, you've been introduced now. Take it from there, if you're interested in him.'

Later, Janine was to laugh at herself for that remark and the nonchalance with which she had made it. She had thought she did not have a jealous bone in her body, that if Suzie or anyone else should wish to make a play for Nikolai it would not affect her one iota. That was what she thought, until she went downstairs and found Gloria Warwick dancing with him . . .

Dancing with him? She was coiled around him like a snake, her hands around his neck, her fingers in the crisp, black curls of his hair. Janine was irritated by the sight of it, telling herself it was not their dancing together which bothered her so much as Gloria's craftiness. She had deliberately excused herself from Janine and Suzie to take the opportunity of approaching Nikolai while the coast was clear! It was pretty obvious who had asked whom to dance.

Or was it?

No sooner had she thought this, and registered that the whole issue bothered her more than it should, when the music came to an end and Nikolai detached himself from Gloria and came over to her. He took two glassses of champagne from a waitress circulating with a tray, and the look on his face was one of distaste. 'If there's one thing I can't stand it's an aggressive female. Who is that creature?'

Janine bit her cheeks. 'One of the gang. You didn't *have* to ask her to dance . . .'

'I was accosted by her!' Nikolai corrected. 'Within earshot of several people, she asked me to dance with her. I was put—I can't remember the English idiom.'

'On the spot,' Janine provided. 'I wonder what her boy-friend thought about that?'

'If he has any sense, he'd have walked out.'

Janine shoook her head. 'He's over there. He's crazy about her. She's a very beautiful girl.'

'That's a matter of opinion. It's certainly her opinion.'

Janine laughed softly. 'Gloria's turned many a man's head, Nikolai. There's something about her——'

'Not this man.'

'Ah, well, you—you're a little different.' She was still smiling because she was privately pleased at Nikolai's total lack of interest in Gloria Warwick—very pleased. And Gloria's performance on the dance floor had made it obvious that she wasn't merely inviting him to dance with her!

Nikolai looked at her curiously. 'Different? I'm not sure what you mean by that.'

She shrugged. 'I mean you've yet to meet the woman who can turn your head, isn't that so?'

He grinned, shaking his head at her. 'If you're asking whether I've ever suffered from that state of lack of control which you refer to as being "in love", the answer is no.' He took the glass from her hand and put it, and his own, on a nearby table. 'Come on, if we have to stay here a respectable length of time, I'm going to make the most of it.'

He led her outside to the patio where several couples were dancing, his hands moving lightly around her waist. 'Ah, now the evening had taken a turn for the better.'

It was fatal, their dancing together. Janine's first instinct was to cut and run—because more than anything she wanted to move closer to Nikolai, to slide her arms around his neck just as Gloria had done. But to do that would be to risk giving him exactly the same message Gloria had given him, and that was certainly not her intention. Still, that was how he would interpret it, and coming from her the invitation would not be refused. Of that she was sure.

No, she dared not do what she wanted to do. As it was, she was acutely aware of him. As it was, she was near enough to catch the faint tang of his aftershave. Her hands were resting on his shoulders; his hands were flat against her rib cage, at her waist, and this alone was causing her pulses to pound, making her entire body scintillatingly alive.

And then his eyes started to caress her—at least, that was how it felt. They moved slowly from her face to her throat, to the curve of her shoulders and on to the soft swell of her breasts in the plunging neckline.

Janine gasped silently, feeling as though he had actually trailed this path with his fingers, and the indigo eyes went immediately back to hers, his voice rather brusque as he spoke. 'To hell with it,' he said. 'Janine, go and get your wrap. I'll make our excuses to our hosts.'

Nonplussed at his first, cryptic, remark, she did as he said without questioning him, without protest. After collecting her wrap she found him talking to Michael and his parents, and she went over to them, feeling a little guilty for leaving early.

But Michael looked more anxious than upset. She reached for him, kissing him briefly on the cheek as she thanked him and his parents for a lovely time. 'It was a super party, thank you.'

His arms came around her. 'I'll see you soon, darling. Take care.' It wasn't his words but the way his arms lingered around her that told her of his reluctance to hand her over to Nikolai.

When they got into the car she was still feeling a little guilty about Michael. Oh, Michael, she thought helplessly, why do you have to be so ... why couldn't you be more ... more *everything!*

Her eyes slid almost unwillingly to Nikolai as he fired the engine and pulled away smoothly, the Sabre moving off like a sleek white arrow into the night. They didn't talk, and Nikolai drove purposefully, a look of concentration on his face while he zipped along the winding lanes as if he knew them intimately.

'Nikolai, you've missed the turning. Go back a hundred yards, you want——'

'I want to talk to you. Somewhere private.'

'Is—is something wrong?' When he didn't answer, she said, 'I'm sorry you didn't enjoy the party.'

Again he said nothing, and it made her feel vaguely alarmed. She decided she'd better wait until he had parked before saying anything else.

The 'somewhere private' turned out to be a vantage point overlooking St Clement's Bay. There was not a car, not a soul around for miles. The only movement outside the Sabre was the swish of the sea.

Nikolai turned off the engine and took hold of her hand. 'I hope I didn't spoil your evening. You wanted to stay longer, didn't you?'

'No,' she said truthfully.

'The problem was, is,' he amended, reaching for her, 'that I don't like all and sundry knowing what's in my mind. And if we'd continued dancing it would have become very obvious . . . I've been wanting to kiss you all evening . . .'

'Nikolai, I——' Janine put her hands flat against his chest, resisting him but knowing it was only a token resistance. 'You said you wanted to talk.'

'I lied,' he said simply, smiling as he caught hold of her hands and put them around his neck, bringing his mouth down to hers.

This time she didn't even try to resist. She, too, had been waiting all evening for this, she had wanted so much to feel his arms around her, to run her fingers through the crispness of his hair. He kissed her passionately, finding an equal response in her as her lips parted to allow the intimate exploration of his tongue.

She yielded to the sheer pleasure of it, her hands sliding inside his jacket, moving over the hard strength of his back. But she knew she was playing with fire, that this physical attraction was something beyond her experience, that she must call a halt now, *now*. She was not safe here, here in the privacy of the car with no one around and no light save that of the full moon.

But the kiss went on and on, then Nikolai's lips moved lightly over her face, touching at the corners of her eyes, her mouth, trailing along her neck and her throat until they were brushing along the firm swell of her breasts. 'Nikolai, no! That's enough!'

He pulled away from her, totally in control, though the quality of his voice told her of his arousal. 'Relax, darling. I have no intention of making love to you on the back seat of a car. That's not my style.' He slid his hands around the back of her neck, pulling her gently towards him, so close that he was almost touching her lips as he spoke. 'Let's go to a hotel, we'll find somewhere warm and luxurious where we can make love. Let's get this thing out of our systems.'

Janine could hardly believe what she had heard. Her disappointment was enormous, so great the tears sprang instantly to her eyes. Go to a hotel? How could he possibly think she would just ... just ... So he thought it was as simple as that! How—how *businesslike* could you get?

Very calmly, very quietly, she said, 'I see. Let's get on with it, you mean? You think this is something that has to be done. Like—like an itch that needs to be scratched? Like a bill that has to be paid!'

He frowned, a hint of concern creeping into his eyes. 'I would never put it so crudely, Janine. All I'm saying is that you want me just as much as I want you.'

Dammit, he was right about that. He was right! His hand had moved to her throat, his fingers moving lightly in a rhythmic, circular movement against her skin as he spoke to her. Janine's breathing had deepened, her pulses were throbbing and he knew it, and there was nothing she could do to stop what was happening to her body, what his very nearness did to her.

But she was in no danger of giving in to it. His— invitation—had brought her down to earth with a crash, and her mind was very much in control. She was hurt, very hurt, by his presumption. 'Life—these things are not so cut and dried to me, Nikolai. The answer is no.' Her voice had risen slightly as some of the hurt showed through.

'Then come to Paris next Friday. I'll pick you up at the airport and we'll spend the week-end together.'

She pulled away from him sharply, staring at him. He didn't understand what she was saying! He was talking about his apartment now, his apartment in Paris ... 'What's this all about, Nikolai?' she asked bitterly. 'Have you got a vacancy at the moment? Is that it?'

He just laughed at her, pulling her tightly against him

so that her breasts were pressing against his chest. 'What the devil are you taking about, you little tease ...'

He bit softly into her shoulder, and Janine's gasp was a mixture of pleasure and pain. 'Let go of me! Let—I'm talking about your mistresses, damn you! I have it on good authority that you keep three of them! Surely you're not in need of a fourth!'

But he still wasn't taking her seriously, and her struggles seemed to excite him further. He kept one arm tightly around her, his free hand moving down the neckline of her dress as he murmured against her ear. 'Lara, I presume. Come on, darling, three of them? All at the same time? Wouldn't you say that's a slight exaggeration?'

'Stop that! *Stop* it!' All the hurt turned to anger and the threat of tears intensified.

He let go of her—finally. Only now was he beginning to take her seriously. 'Janine, what—what's wrong? What do you expect me to say? I enjoy women just as much as the next man, but what Lara's told you is nonsense!' Then he was smiling again, reaching for her. 'I want you, Janine. *You.* You and I are going to be lovers, you know that as well as I. Come on,' he coaxed, 'let's not play games. Let's go to a hotel ...'

Janine's last vestige of control slipped. She slapped him. She slapped him hard. 'You insult me, Nikolai! Worse, you succeed in making me feel cheap!'

'Cheap?' He stared at her in disbelief. 'I—Dear God, you mean it, don't you?'

She swallowed hard, turning her head away, fighting with everything in her not to let the tears spill over.

Nikolai got hold of her almost roughly, turning her around in her seat. 'You really mean it!' He took her face between his hands, probing the depths of her eyes more deeply than he ever had before. Her tears did not spill over but they were there, glistening, unmistakable.

He let go of her abruptly as if her skin had suddenly burned his fingers, and he spoke only after several seconds' silence, his voice very, very quiet. 'Cheap? You? No, never that, Janine.'

Without another word he fired the engine and stuck the gear lever into reverse, swinging the Sabre on to the road in a manner which was reckless compared to the way he normally drove.

But he wasn't angry. Quite what he was feeling, thinking, she had no way of knowing.

Silence reigned. He wanted an affair with her and she had refused. Surely there was, simply, nothing to say?

She wasn't angry, either. Not now. She just felt an overwhelming disappointment—a disappointment she could make little sense of. It wasn't as if she could blame him for his assumption, in honesty. She had responded to him so readily, so hungrily . . . Yes, she wanted him. But to have an affair with Nikolai would be like travelling a road to . . . nowhere. Precisely nowhere.

She did not have time to analyse that thought. They were home. The house was in darkness and they let themselves in quietly. Janine flicked on the downstairs light in the hall. 'Would—would you like a drink? Or a coffee?'

For long seconds Nikolai just looked down at her. 'I'm sorry, what did you say?'

'I—said would you like a drink?'

'No. Thank you, no, I'll call it a night.' He seemed totally preoccupied. Then, just as he reached the stairs, 'Janine, I——' But he changed his mind, shook his head. 'Goodnight.'

'Goodnight.'

She forced herself to move away, not to watch him as he went upstairs. The champagne had left her feeling thirsty and she made a pot of tea and stayed in the kitchen to drink it. Besides, she wouldn't sleep. Not yet.

For almost an hour she lingered before going to her room. She padded quietly, barefooted, to the bathroom, removing her make-up, brushing her hair and her teeth. When she hung up her dress and slipped into her nightie, the silence of the house, her bedroom, seemed to close in on her and for some obscure reason she felt an acute sense of depression.

But the reason did not remain obscure for long. Not even attempting to sleep, she switched off the overhead light and flicked on her bedside lamp, settling in the armchair by the windows. She opened the curtains a chink, just enough so she could feel the breeze from the open window.

It was only then that she understood the thought that had run through her mind earlier—that having an affair with Nikolai would be like travelling a road to nowhere. During the past hour, she had re-lived the entire evening, enjoyed it all over again, from the look on Nikolai's face when she had come into the living room, dressed up, ready for the party, to the moment when everything was spoiled by that scene in the car, when it had all got out of hand. For her, at least, it had all gone too far.

A road to nowhere? Yes. And she had already, unwittingly, taken the first step. She liked Nikolai Nekrassov far more than was good for her, far more than she should. Against all the odds, this had happened; she not only liked him but respected him. Now, she had even to admire his honesty, his directness in making it plain to her what he wanted. Distasteful though she found it, at least he had been honest.

And he never said what he didn't mean, either. That was something else she could be sure of about him. On their first evening here, in Jersey, while he had changed his mind about Lara and Robbie, he would make no apology for the harsh things he had said in Lille, making it clear that he had meant what he'd said at the time.

He was, all in all, quite a—what? Extraordinary man? The most exciting, interesting man she had ever met? The only man who had ever made her feel so startlingly, deliciously, *alive*, utterly feminine and glad of it?

But why think in euphemistic terms when what she really meant was that it would be easy, oh so easy, to fall in love with him. And *that* was the road to nowhere.

Because Nikolai Nekrassov was not capable of that particular kind of love. He didn't even believe in it.

But Janine had taken only the first step along the

road, and she had seen all the warning signs, the danger signals, in time. Luckily she was not——

The knock on her door was quiet, but in the silence of her room it sounded loud in her ears. She shot to her feet, startled, closing the chink in the curtains. Was it Nikolai? Or was it her mother? It was probably Rose, Rose with her over-developed maternal instincts, wanting to make sure that her daughter, adult though she was, was home and safe.

Even as she wondered who had knocked, Janine was putting on her negligee and heading for the door. She had no choice but to answer; her light would be showing, so it was obvious she wasn't asleep.

It was Nikolai.

He was half dressed, barefooted, wearing the trousers to the suit he had had on, the blue shirt open halfway to his waist revealing a broad and darkly hirsute chest. 'Take it easy.' He spoke quickly, quietly, as he saw her look of alarm.

He stepped into the room, obliging her to move out of his way as he closed the door, because she was not going to stop him, to argue—there was no way she wanted to risk waking her parents. Again he told her to relax. 'It's all right,' he assured her. 'I want to talk to you, that's all.'

He crossed the room and sat on her bed; Janine sat in the chair she had been occupying, pulling her negligee more closely around her. She was not even aware of doing this until he smiled, a wry smile. 'I couldn't sleep for thinking about you, Janine. I believe I've made an incredibly stupid mistake about you.'

It was not a question, it was a statement. She looked at him quickly, at a loss to understand. She was fairly at ease, realising he was not about to make a pass at her. 'What—what do you mean?'

Again his smile was wry. 'I mean you're not what you seem, in spite of your apparent sophistication, in spite of your apparent experience and worldliness. You've responded to me like——' He shook his head slowly, as if he were disappointed in himself, unsure how to say what he wanted to say. 'I'm not going to apologise for wanting you. I did, I do, want to make love to you.' He held up both hands, silencing her. 'But for you it's . . . it's too much, too fast. This attraction between us, it's—too powerful. For you. Yes?'

'I—yes.' She looked down at the carpet, uncomfortably aware of colour rising in her cheeks.

Very quietly he added, 'Not only have you not made love with Granger, you've never had a lover at all.'

Janine couldn't speak, couldn't look at him. She was embarrassed, whether she ought to be or not, she was embarrassed.

'Come here.' Nikolai stood, holding his hands out to her.

'No.' Still she could not bring herself to look at him. She spoke aggressively in an effort to eclipse how she was really feeling. 'If you think this is amusing, let me tell——'

'I don't think it's at all amusing.' Certainly there was no amusement in his voice. There was weariness, so much so that her eyes went immediatly to his. 'I think it's . . . refreshing.' He sighed. 'To one who is world-weary, as you put it so succinctly at the party tonight, that's how it strikes me. Now come here.'

He was holding out his hands again, and she, knowing she could trust him, went to him, allowing him to take her hands. 'As I said, Janine, I make no apology for wanting you. But I'm sorry, very sorry, if I made you feel cheap tonight. That was not my intention.'

'I know. I—it's all right.'

He smiled, seeming genuinely relieved. 'You know, tonight you were a walking aphrodisiac, and now you're all scrubbed and pink and smelling of soap.' He let go of her hands so he could run his fingers through her hair, which was falling softly around her shoulders as she usually wore it. 'And now you look like an angel.'

She laughed. 'That I'm not!'

'I'm glad to hear it!' Nikolai smiled a slow smile, his eyes travelling down the length of her body. 'And you look just as desirable.'

Then his smile faded and his eyes became intense as

they held hers for long seconds as they stood, close but not touching. 'You are . . . an extraordinary, exceptional girl.' Then, almost to himself he added, 'What am I going to do about you? What the hell am I going to do about you?' And with that he left, kissing her gently on the forehead as he went.

Janine sank on to her bed, making no attempt to stop the tears which flooded her eyes. It was time, high time, to stop fooling herself. She wasn't in danger of falling in love with Nikolai, she was already in love with him. Against all the odds, she had fallen in love with her brother's brother-in-law. What were the odds against that happening?

It didn't matter. It had happened. And now that she was finally being honest with herself she might as well admit she had loved him all along, from the very moment she had set eyes on him...

She sat motionless, crying silently.

And where did this leave her? Nowhere. Precisely nowhere.

CHAPTER NINE

THE look on Lara's face on seeing Nikolai at the airport was something Janine would always remember. Under her mop of curly black hair, her face was tanned, animated, vivacious, and when she had spotted Janine and Nikolai, waiting for them, her happiness on seeing her brother was a joy to behold.

Robbie had looked momentarily dubious, even alarmed, before realising that all was well, that Nikolai was obviously here in peace. And that much was obvious because Janine was by Nikolai's side, waving enthusiastically.

The two men had shaken hands, greeted one another only by using first names, but that had been enough to break the ice. Any remaining doubts Robbie might have had were instantly dispelled. For Lara's sake, any hard feelings Robbie might have had had not shown through. But knowing her brother's nature as she did, Janine was sure that Robbie would not harbour hard feelings.

Lara, typically, had almost shrieked her joy, letting everyone in the airport know, several times, what Nikolai's name was as she flung her arms around him.

And now they were all in the Sabre heading for the newlyweds' cottage in Trinity, and Lara was talking ten to the dozen about Portugal, where she and Robbie had spent the last six weeks.

'Darling, I don't think Janine and Nikolai really want to know about the composition of the soil in Portugal.' It was a typical Robbie tease, and Lara rose to it.

'The comp—— Robert, what are you taking about? I'm telling them about the food we had there!'

'That's what I mean! You're going into such detail— I'm wondering what you'll say next about our honeymoon!'

Janine and Nikolai exchanged looks. They all laughed, and then a physical fight, or a tickling session or something, broke out in the back of the car and was accompanied by a lot of feminine giggling—which in turn was followed by a sudden silence.

Janine pressed her lips together as Nikolai glanced in his driving mirror, raising an eyebrow as he did so. Then the indigo eyes flicked to hers and he grinned. 'I must apologise for my sister,' he said loudly. 'Somewhere in her upbringing, I went wrong. Unlike me, she doesn't mind putting on public displays of— whatever!'

It was a good day, a happy day. Robbie and Lara were on cloud nine, Nikolai was in a wonderful mood, and Janine . . . well, Janine was composed, in control.

Fortunately it did not show in her face or her eyes, but she had had no sleep at all the previous night. She had done a great deal of thinking, but she had not cried for long. Oddly enough it was Nikolai's words which had made her pull herself together.

He had referred to being in love as a 'state of lack of control'. On hearing this, Janine had thought it further evidence of how practical his mind was. She would never have thought of it in those terms, but, in the midst of tears, she realised how right he was, and it was then that she had pulled herself together.

The first thing she had decided was that Nikolai must never find out how she really felt about him. She would rather die than have him laugh at the discovery. And that meant she must do her utmost to hide it from her family, too.

The next logical step in her thinking was that she would make things easier for herself if she left Jersey. She had been thinking of doing this is any case; she just hadn't got round to it. Well, she would act positively now. Next week she would ring Pauline Norris and say she was going to accept her offer of sharing the flat. London, a change of work, would provide a distraction and it would also mean she could avoid seeing Nikolai when next he came to visit his sister.

'Janine?' Lara was tapping her on the shoulder. 'What time is Mum expecting us tonight?'

'Around eight o'clock. She realised you'd want time to unpack and take a bath and show Nikolai the cottage.'

They were all dining at Janine's home tonight. Rose was already preparing one of her special dinners and Archie had put some champagne in the fridge and had dusted a few bottles of his best French wine. In the meantime, they would have tea at the cottage and that would give Nikolai a chance to see it, newly decorated and newly furnished as it was.

Janine had bought in the bare essentials for Robbie and Lara, and she was in the kitchen making tea when Lara came down from the bathroom.

'Ooh, that's better!' Lara pushed her fingers through the damp curls of her hair. 'I feel more human now I've bathed.' She nodded towards the living room. 'What are those two talking about?'

'Your new restaurant.'

'Ah! Good.'

Janine smiled. 'Robbie will be signing the lease this week, won't he?'

'*Oui*. And then the workmen will move in and start

the alterations. Robert and I—oh, we'll have a hundred things to do! Organising, hiring, buying, and Nikolai will no doubt be making some constructive suggestions to R——' Lara broke off suddenly. She closed the kitchen door and came over to where Janine was standing, putting biscuits and cakes on plates. 'What have you done to him, Janine?'

'What? Who?'

'Nikolai, of course! He's . . . different.'

'Different? And is that a good thing?' Janine had no idea what Lara meant. 'I mean, is it for the better or for the worse?'

'Oh, Janine! For the better! Assuming he stays like this.'

Janine was putting cups and saucers on a tray now, laughing. 'What *are* you on about?'

To which Lara merely shrugged dramatically, spun around in a full circle and shoved her hands into the pockets of her jeans. 'It's hard to—he's sort of . . . more open, less intense, if you see what I mean.'

Janine didn't. But she wasn't going to press Lara further, she wasn't going to be seen to be too interested.

'It's you,' Lara went on. 'You've had a good influence on him. I mean, why is he here?'

'To see you, of course. To bury the hatchet.'

'The what?' Lara threw back her head and laughed. 'Yes, but *why?* I mean, how come?'

'You're beginning to sound like my father!' The older girl couldn't help laughing. 'Asking why, why, why!'

'Well, whatever you said to him that day in Lille, it worked. It might have had a delayed reaction, but it worked!' Lara scooped up the tea tray, and Janine opened the kitchen door for her.

'Tea's up!' Lara said to the men, sounding just like Rose, delighted to be hostess for the first time in her new home.

Janine watched Nikolai watching Lara, and she realised how stupid she had been when once she had thought he didn't love his sister. Brotherly love, at least, was something he was capable of. There was tenderness in his eyes now, a look she had never seen before.

'So, Nikolai Andreivitch, when did you get here? Yesterday?' asked Lara. 'Will you be staying till Monday morning?'

'Would you be interested in taking a look round the island?' Robbie put in. 'And how are you getting on with my parents, by the way?'

'Extremely well, Robert.' Nikolai's eyes moved to Janine, sitting next to him on the settee. 'And with your sister. I've been here a week, in fact, and Janine has kept me company and shown me the island.' He paused, seeing the look of surprise on his sister's face.

'You've been here a *week*?' Lara couldn't seem to believe it. 'You've taken a whole week off work?' She turned to Janine. 'I told you you've had a good influence on him! And this proves it! Nikolai very rarely takes time off work—very rarely. He's always worked too hard, just like our father did. He puts in twelve hours a day at the factory and the only time he doesn't work is at the week-ends. At the week-ends he——'

'Lara.' The word came mildly from the Frenchman, but there was a note of warning in it.

Lara, however, was not easily silenced. 'We're among family, I can say what I like.' She turned back to Janine. 'At the week-ends he has some relaxation. Or should I say fun?' Her gorgeous blue eyes were sparkling with laughter. 'That's when he makes time for his sex life!'

'I . . . see.' Janine manufactured a smile. She heard Nikolai let out an impatient breath, and knowing that he knew what she was now thinking turned her smile into a genuine one. She almost sympathised with him. Oh, Lara! she thought, if you only knew what you'd said! 'Well, I—I'm glad to hear Nikolai has some relaxation in life.'

'When do you have to go back?' asked Robbie, bringing the conversation back to its original point.

'I'm sailing tomorrow.'

'Oh, Nikolai!' Lara was disappointed. 'I don't think much of your timing. You've been here a week while I was away, and now you tell me you're leaving tomorrow!'

'I'm sorry,' shrugged Nikolai. 'I have a business meeting first thing Monday morning. It is important, Lara.'

'Then you must come over again soon.'

Robbie got to his feet. 'Well, now the bathroom's free I can show you the rest of the cottage, Nikolai. We have all of three rooms up there—including the bathroom!'

Dinner that evening was superb. Rose had excelled herself and was lavished with compliments. It was for the kitchen—and Rose—that Lara made a beeline as soon as they got to the house and it was Lara and Rose who together cleared the table after dinner and did the washing up, allowing no one else to have a hand in the work.

It was also a rather noisy dinner—though very enjoyable. Lara regaled everyone with her and Robbie's adventures of the past six weeks, rising time and time again to her husband's teasing, and to Archie's, while Rose encouraged her always with things like, 'Go on, darling, tell us more.'

The newlyweds left at midnight, not because they particularly wanted to but because they were tired, and Nikolai and Janine had a final—and quiet—cup of coffee with her parents before they went to bed.

'Well, I'm off to bed.' Archie tapped out his pipe in the ashtray and got to his feet. 'Are you coming, Rose?'

'Yes. You're not leaving till noon tomorrow, are you?' she asked Nikolai.

Nikolai stood up as Rose stood up. 'No. But Robbie and Lara are taking me to see the restaurant in the morning, so I'm afraid I won't see you after breakfast. I'll drive straight to the port after I've seen the restaurant.'

He took Rose's hand and raised it to his lips. Then he shook hands with Archie. 'I want to thank you both for your hospitality. If you ever feel like spending a weekend in Lille, my home is at your disposal.'

Rose was beaming. 'Thank you. And it was lovely having you here, Nikolai.'

'You're more than welcome, any time,' said Archie. 'But we'll say our goodbyes at breakfast. Goodnight.'

'I'll say goodnight, too.' Janine lingered only for a moment after her parents left the room.

Nikolai was still standing, and looked at her quickly. 'You're going to bed?'

'Of course. I'm shattered.' She was, too, because she hadn't slept the night before. But he didn't know that.

'I—was going to suggest we went for a drive.'

There was something on his mind; Janine had been aware of it all evening. He had grown progressively quieter as the hours passed, not that he volunteered much in company in any case. But he had been . . . too quiet.

Nevertheless, there was no way she wanted to end up in the privacy of his car with him when it was pitch dark outside. She got up, stretching, keeping her voice light. 'Count me out, Count Nikolai,' she said laughingly. 'I'm too tired.'

He smiled at the play on words. Then he crossed the room in a flash and caught hold of her by the waist. 'If you're going to insist on staying . . . as sweet as you are . . . then don't do things like that.'

She looked up at him, affected instantly by the feel of his arms around her. But she had no idea what he meant. 'Like what?'

'Like stretching laguorously, like wearing a white silk blouse I can see through, like smiling at me over a candlelit dinner table . . .'

'Oh, Nikolai, really!' She laughed it off. 'So that's why you suggested a drive! You were going to reissue your invitation to your bachelor pad in Paris!'

'No.' He was even more serious now. He let go of her. 'I wasn't going to do that.' He sat down and took out his box of cheroots and his lighter. 'I was going to talk about Lara, actually.'

Janine sat down again, facing him. It was most unusual to see him smoking again. He normally had just one after his meal, and that was it. 'You still have your misgivings?'

'No. On the contrary.'

'Then why do you look so—disturbed?'

'Because it was only today, tonight, that I realised how much my sister has missed out on. I told you she's had everything she's wanted in life, that she's been spoiled. That's what I thought—but how wrong I was! She's gone short of a great deal . . . warmth, love. Oh, I love her, she's a sweet girl, but I'm not a demonstrative man and I've—perhaps been too strict with her.'

Janine's smile was tinged with sadness. She wanted to go over to him, to put her arms around him because suddenly he looked—lonely. That was the only word she could think of, strange though it seemed. But she stayed where she was. 'Nikolai, you've done a good job with Lara, evidently. As you say, she's a lovely girl, a nice person. You couldn't be all things to her, you couldn't have taken the place of her mother as well as her father. You're only one person, Nikolai . . . just a man.'

'Just a man.' He echoed her words quietly, his deep blue eyes looking at her intently now. Then he repeated the words again, seeming to give them more meaning than Janine had intended.

There was silence for several seconds before he spoke again, looking away from her as he did so. 'Your mother, your parents, are wonderful with her. So is Robert, of course.'

'They all love her. She's responding to it, naturally. She's——'

'Positively blooming, as the English might put it.' He smiled then but there was something self-deprecating about it. 'It would seem that my eighteen-year-old sister has more wisdom than I have.'

'What do you mean?'

'I mean that she's recognised, and made up for, what's been lacking in her life—which is more than I've done. She's found the important things in life, too.'

Janine wasn't sure what to say to that. She wasn't sure how she should respond to him in this mood, a most unusual mood. 'But there's nothing lacking in your life, surely?'

It was some time before Nikolai answered that, and when he did so his answer was frustratingly cryptic. 'I didn't think so, but this week——' He stopped abruptly.

Janine frowned. 'This week—what?'

The living room door opened and Rose appeared, looking nonplussed. 'Oh! I'm sorry, I didn't realise you were chatting!' She looked from Nikolai to Janine, her face breaking into a smile. 'I thought you'd gone to bed, I came down for my spectacles. Your father is reading, so I thought I'd do the same for an hour . . .'

She picked up her glasses from the coffee table, apologising again as she left the room.

'Nikolai? You were saying?' Janine tried to pick up the threads of their conversation, but she saw at once that it was no use. His attitude had changed. In fact it was he who was stretching now.

'Yes,' he said lazily, casually. 'I was saying that this week has been hectic. But enjoyable,' he added with a smile. 'Thank you, Janine. It was—very enjoyable.'

Very enjoyable—that was all it had been to him. But for her it had been . . . She shrugged. 'My pleasure. Goodnight. Nikolai.'

She went to bed then, she didn't dare to stay any longer in his company lest she gave something away, lest he saw how desperately sad she was feeling because he was leaving in the morning.

'He's not at all the devil you took him for, eh, Jan?'

Janine and her father were weaving their way through the traffic in St Helier, on their way to work. It was Nikolai whom Archie was referring to, Nikolai he'd been talking about since breakfast.

It was Monday, and only this morning had Janine learned that during the previous week Nikolai had given her father a cheque for the wedding expenses and, this time, Archie had accepted it.

'Jan?'

'No, not at all. In fact he's . . . very likeable, once you get to know him.'

Archie gave her a sideways look as he pulled away from the traffic lights. 'You're not cross because I accepted that cheque? You see, not only did he insist but——'

'But it would have—sort of alienated him if you'd refused again. He wanted to pay for his sister's wedding, to have a hand in it somehow, so you accepted.'

'Precisely. I accepted gracefully, and it had nothing to do with money.'

'I know, Dad, I know.' Janine looked at her father lovingly. He was wise and understanding and he knew a great deal about human nature. Very casually she asked, 'What did you make of Nikolai, actually?'

Archie spoke without hesitation. 'He's the type who makes the best kind of friend and the worst kind of enemy. I'll bet he's a bastard in business, and he should never, ever, be underestimated . . .'

Janine's eyebrows went up.

'. . . He's been too strict in Lara's upbringing, but love and concern were his motives. He is, he will be, fiercely protective of those he loves, and I can tell you now that there's no way he would have cut Lara out of his life permanently, despite what he told you in Lille.' He broke off, grinning. 'We've all been given the once-over, and he approves.'

Janine was staring at him. 'So . . . does all this mean you like him or not?'

'But of course! Enormously! He's straightforward, a man of principle, honest.'

With a nonchalant wave of her arm, Janine said, 'Mm. He's certainly got a practical sort of mind—but I'm not sure that he's straightforward.'

Archie chuckled. 'Ah, well, he won't volunteer what's going through his mind, but he'll give you an honest answer if you ask him. He doesn't trust easily, he's not impressed easily, he's far older than his years and he's extremely intelligent. An old soul, you might say.' He finished with a flourish, seeming pleased with his analysis. 'All in all, he's very straightforward, as I said.'

It was time to change the subject, Janine thought, otherwise her father would start asking *why* she was showing this interest in Nikolai. 'Oh, by the way, Dad, I phoned Pauline Norris early this morning. She's coming over to stay with her parents for a few days at Easter.'

'That's nice.'

'Mm. Actually, there's something I want to talk to her about. You know she's keen on the idea of my moving in with her . . .'

Archie was not surprised. He finished his daughter's sentence for her. 'And you're thinking about doing just that.'

'I'm thinking about it,' Janine said casually.

She had, in fact, told Pauline of her decision—though not of the reason for it. That could not be discussed by telephone; it would have to wait until Pauline came to Jersey. But she was being cautious with her father, not wanting to spring it on him too suddenly. She had decided that the best thing would be to let her parents know she was now thinking seriously of moving to England, and then some time next week she would present it as a positive decision. She didn't want to leave it any longer than that because she would have to stay on at the travel agency for a while in any case—to give Archie time to find a replacement.

The family took it well. Janine waited until the following week-end and then she made her announcement. They were all at Lara and Robbie's—enjoying Lara's first home-cooked Sunday roast, the cooking of which, Lara pointed out proudly, had been done entirely by herself and not with the help of the chef she was married to.

'I can't really see you settling in London, Jan.' That was Robbie's opinion. 'I mean, you're more of a country girl than a city girl.'

'Far more,' Rose agreed. 'But Jan's never settled since she came back from Switzerland, have you, darling?' She was disappointed but philosophical about it. 'And I suppose this is something you'll have to get out of your system—wanderlust, I call it. It's something all my children have grown up with . . .'

It's Nikolai Nekrassov, to be more precise, Janine thought painfully. And how long will it take me to forget him? How long? Could she, would she be able to?

'Oh, I'll miss you so much, Janine!' Lara put in dramatically but very sincerely.

Robbie looked heavenward, laughing. 'Hey, she's only going to London, not Australia! She can pop home—door to door—in less than a couple of hours. And don't forget,' he added, turning to his sister, 'we'll be having a party when we open the restaurant. Keep that week-end free.'

'I will,' Janine grinned, 'when I know what date it'll be!' That was, as yet, by no means certain. There was quite a bit of work to be done on Robbie's premises.

Lara was looking glum, unconvinced. 'People say that, Robert, when they leave home—that they'll visit often. But they don't. Janine will get caught up in her new life and we'll be lucky if we see her twice a year. Once a year!'

Janine smiled at her sister-in-law. 'You'll see me more often than that,' she promised. But not, she added to herself, on the week-ends when your brother is visiting . . .

'I shall hold you to that,' warned Lara. 'Anyway,' she brightened suddenly, getting up from the dinner table, 'Nikolai is keeping to his word. He promised he'd come back and see us soon . . .' She was fishing in a magazine rack for a newspaper, and Janine's stomach contracted nervously. She wanted to shout at Lara, demand to know what she was talking about.

'He's coming over next week-end——' Lara went on.

'Next week-end?' Janine couldn't help herself. She had not, absolutely not, expected this! She hadn't dreamt that Nikolai would be back so soon . . .

'It's Easter!' Lara said happily. 'He's coming on Friday morning and he's staying for two nights. Oh!' Her hand went to her mouth and she looked quickly at Rose and Archie. 'I hope that's all right? Robbie thought it would be—I mean, I only spoke to Nikolai this morning and——'

'It's perfectly all right!' Rose assured her.

'I told him he was welcome any time,' Archie put in, speaking for the first time in a long time. 'And I meant it.'

Janine groaned inwardly. Nikolai would be staying at her house. The newlyweds had only one spare bedroom, and it was the one room in the house they had not furnished. Since the new restaurant was gobbling up their financial resources, they'd thought it pointless to furnish a guest room when it wouldn't be all that long before they might decide to use it as a nursery . . .

'What's the newspaper for?' Archie was speaking to Lara, but it was Janine he was glancing at. She groaned again, almost audibly this time, afraid that her facial expression might have given some of her thoughts away.

So Nikolai was coming on Good Friday. That was this coming Friday . . . She would have to make herself scarce, spend as much time with Pauline as she could.

Things got worse. Lara opened the French newspaper she had plonked on the table, folded it in half and handed it to her father-in-law. 'It isn't the first time Nikolai's been mentioned in the paper, but he's never been mentioned in a gossip column before! Take a look at that!'

Janine didn't want to look. But the paper was passed from one person to the next and she had no choice. The newspaper was dated the previous day, Saturday, and in it there was a full-length photograph of Nikolai—with a tall, slender blonde on his arm. He was dressed immaculately in an evening suit and the blonde was stunningly attractive and wearing a low-cut gown and what appeared to be a mink jacket draped casually around her shoulders.

'It's she who's attracted the attention of the press,' Lara informed everyone. 'See what it says? She's the daughter of a millionaire banker and she's been engaged three times.'

There was no article about the couple in the photograph, just a caption beneath it which speculated, audaciously, *'Another potential husband for Michelle Duval?'* There were just a couple of lines underneath the caption saying who the girl's father was, that Nikolai was Chairman and Managing Director of Sabre Cars of Lille and that the couple had been attending the Opera the previous evening.

Janine handed the paper to Robbie.

So Nikolai was in Paris this week-end—as usual. Here she was, having fallen deeply in love with him, nervous at the very prospect of seeing him again. And there he was, in Paris with a beautiful blonde, getting his . . . fun . . . in life, as Lara had put it. *Making time for his sex life.*

Janine felt sick. It was just as well they had all finished eating, otherwise she would never have managed to do justice to Lara's roast.

CHAPTER TEN

JANINE got into Michael's car at eleven-thirty on Good Friday morning. She had made up her mind that she was not going to be sitting at home when Nikolai arrived. He was flying to the island this time, which meant he would not have his wheels with him, and Robbie and Lara had gone to collect him at the airport.

'To what do I owe this honour?' Michael looked at her a little uncertainly as he started his car. 'When a beautiful girl rings me and asks me to take her to lunch,' he teased, 'I can't help thinking that maybe . . .'

'That maybe she has nothing better to do,' Janine finished with her stock answer.

They laughed, though Janine was actually feeling sad as she looked at Michael, wondering why it was that one man had the power to excite her even when they were miles apart while another man, dear to her though he was, attractive though he was, could do nothing to stir her senses.

And it was no exaggeration that Nikolai could excite her even from a distance. She had thought about him constantly since he had left the island and it was still there—her ability to see every detail of his face merely by closing her eyes when thinking about him. These days, however, she conjured up his image because she wanted to, whereas before she had tried for months on end to rid him from her mind. Tried and failed.

'Actually, I want to talk to you,' she said to Michael.

'Sounds promising!' He glanced at her, but Janine wasn't saying anything else for the moment.

She had to tell Michael that she was moving to London; he knew nothing about it yet because she hadn't seen him since she made her decision. But it should really make no difference to him; he should know by now that she was a lost cause, that there was no hope of their ever getting together. There never had been.

They drove inland and ordered drinks in a bar-restaurant which was off the beaten track, frequented more by local people than tourists . . . But Michael was more upset by Janine's news than she had expected him to be.

'But why? Why?' This was his first question, and Janine had anticipated it.

'Well, you know I've never settled properly since I came home from working abroad.'

'But——' He frowned, his disappointment suddenly changing to annoyance. 'It's something to do with him, isn't it?'

'Who?'

'Come off it, darling. The Russian, the Frenchman, whatever the hell he is.'

'It has nothing whatever to do with him.' Unfortunately, she could not tell him that her leaving Jersey was partially—mainly—to do with Nikolai. She wanted to be completely honest with Michael, but she dared not, she couldn't risk him telling Robbie or Lara, she couldn't risk their hinting of it to Nikolai. She might be doing everyone concerned an injustice in thinking such information would be passed on, but it was a chance she was in no way prepared to take.

If Nikolai had even an inkling of her feelings for him, he would think her idiotic—the unrealistic romantic he had so often accused her of being.

'Michael, surely you can understand it? I'm just bored, that's all. I need a change. I'm sick of going to the same places with the same people.'

'Me included.'

'Michael——'

He sighed deeply, resignedly, covering her hand with his own. 'It's all right, Jan. You've told me over and over again to give up on you. You never believed that I'm in love with you, did you? But it's true.' He picked up his drink and finished it in one swallow, signalling for the waiter to bring him another. 'Well, your message has finally got through. I—good luck, Jan. Whatever it is you're looking for, whatever it is you want, I hope you find it.'

She found what she wanted when she got home in the middle of the afternoon. He was sitting in the garden with the rest of the family and he got to his feet when Janine appeared.

He greeted her in the French fashion, kissing both of her cheeks, and she smiled at him, masking with her casualness the effect he had on her. 'Nikolai! It's nice to see you again, did you have a good trip?'

She saw a slight frown pulling at his eyebrows and she felt the intense scrutiny of the indigo eyes so acutely that she had to look away. She was on view, not only to him but to her family.

'I did.' The deep voice compelled her eyes back to his. 'And you had an enjoyable lunch with . . . Michael Granger?'

Everyone started chatting at once, it seemed. Robbie was asking why she hadn't brought Michael in for tea, Lara said something about the plans she'd made for tomorrow—and within five minutes Janine was to find that her own plans for the rest of today had gone awry. She discovered this when, in front of everyone, Nikolai invited her out to dinner. Or rather, when he *told* her he was taking her out to dinner.

She was sitting opposite him, on one of the garden hammocks, next to her father. 'Oh, that would have been nice, Nikolai, but I'm afraid I can't. I'm going out with a girl friend tonight. Besides, you're here to see Lara.'

'I shall spend the whole of tomorrow with Lara,' he replied, his eyes travelling the length of her body.

Fortunately no one else was taking any notice, they were chatting among themselves—except for Archie. 'I'm afraid Pauline can't make it tonight,' her father told her. 'She phoned just after you'd gone out with Michael. She's gone over to Guernsey this afternoon and she's staying the night there, with her aunt. Her parents have gone too, of course. Anyway, she said she'll ring you when she gets back in the morning to make arrangements to see you. She's hoping you can spend the day with her.'

Janine was cursing inwardly, but she coped beautifully. 'I see . . .' She turned to Nikolai, turning her hands palms upwards. 'Then I'm free.'

He said nothing else for the moment. He just nodded.

She had had no choice but to accept, in the circumstances. To be obvious in avoiding Nikolai's company would be to arouse curiosity, for he was, after all, one of the family and, ostensibly, a friend. She did not want questions of any kind to be asked.

Later, as she was getting ready to go out, she paused for a moment to look at the photographs she and Nikolai had taken a couple of weeks earlier. Click. And there was Nikolai, on the beach, where they had strolled hand in hand and discussed French philosophers. Click. And there she was, mounting a horse at the local stables when they had gone riding. Click, click, and there they were standing outside Mont Orgueil Castle . . .

She put the photos in her handbag, intending to show them to Nikolai later. In truth she was feeling both excited and nervous at the prospect of spending the evening alone with him, and she prayed that she would cope as well as she wanted to cope—with a friendly detachment which would hide her true feelings.

Her prayers were answered. Janine coped with complete success and in view of the surprise that the evening held in store for her, that was nothing short of remarkable.

They were in her car, Nikolai was driving, and they had been travelling for ten minutes before it occurred to her to ask what sort of restaurant he would like to eat in.

'That's all been taken care of,' he told her, smiling, 'Archie suggested earlier that I should book a table in view of the influx of Easter holidaymakers.'

But there were few holidaymakers in the restaurant. It was a small, intimate place which was wildly expensive and specialised in French cuisine. As she and Nikolai were shown to a corner, candlelit table, Janine felt decidedly uneasy. Nikolai must have told her father what sort of place he wanted to take her to; how else would he have known where to find a restaurant like this? Apart from that, she felt unsuitably dressed in a simple pale green shift.

'I—wish I'd asked you earlier where we were going. I'd have worn something more appropriate.' She took the handwritten menu the waiter was offering her and glanced at Nikolai uncertainly.

When the waiter was out of earshot, he said, 'You look beautiful, Janine. No matter what you are wearing. That's because you are beautiful.'

He was searching her eyes. The candle flickered, reminding her of something he had said to her on their last evening together.

'Have you no smile for me this evening?' he asked, almost as if he had read her mind.

'I—remember the warning you gave me.'

His smile was slow, wicked, and the deep blue eyes lit up with amusement. 'You do well to,' he said quietly. 'Because I need very little encouragement as far as you're concerned.'

She turned her attention to the menu, feeling warm in spite of the thinness of her dress. While she was telling Nikolai what she would like to eat, she was telling herself she must be on guard. His charm, his attentiveness, his attractiveness in the dark suit he was wearing were all combining to make her feel slightly intoxicated. This, before a single drop of wine had passed her lips.

She thought of the tall, slender blonde in the newspaper photograph and reminded herself that he had been through this routine with *her* only last weekend. He was, as Michael had once warned her, slick. A practised seducer of women. And wasn't it human nature to want something even more—when that something was being denied to you?

He gave his orders to the waiter and the wine waiter and then the inquisition, the *trauma*, began. 'Now, what's all this I hear about your going to live in London?'

She blinked in surprise at his tone of voice. 'What's to tell? I want a change. I'm bored.'

'With what—exactly?'

'With my life style, with my work in the travel agency, with the island.'

'But you like the island.'

'Mm. But like I say, I want a change.' She paused, having to think quickly. 'I want more excitement in life than the island can offer, and in London I'll find all the variety I could want—theatres, shows, clubs, you know the sort of thing,' she shrugged. 'This has been on the cards for some time, Nikolai.'

He grunted. 'Archie tells me you've never been settled since you came back from Switzerland, but I'm wondering whether it's occurred to you——'

She frowned. 'Go on.'

'It doesn't matter.' The waiter had arrived with their hors d'oeuvres.

Silence reigned for quite a time and it was not until their plates were cleared that he said, 'We have a lot in common, you and I. We've proved that, if you'll think about it. We like driving, riding, tennis, life outdoors generally and . . .' he glanced around the restaurant, '. . . evenings such as this.'

She just looked at him, having no idea what was coming as he continued in a matter of fact tone. 'I've been doing a lot of thinking during the past couple of weeks, Janine, and I've—I want you to marry me.'

There was no way on earth that she could have hidden her shock. She jumped visibly, her mouth opening in astonishment.

'Now why are you looking at me like that?' he enquired, as if she had no reason to be surprised. 'I've been taking stock of my life lately, as you obviously have, and I think it's time I settled down, made a few changes. I want you to share my life.'

Janine could not have spoken if she had wanted to, if she had known what to say. Fortunately she didn't have to try, because two waiters descended upon the table and started serving the main course. She watched them as they piled food on to her plate, her head spinning in confusion. She didn't know whether to laugh or to cry.

So Nikolai thought he should make a few changes in his life, that he should settle down with someone—and he had dipped his hand into a hat and pulled out her name! It could just as easily have been the name of the blonde he was out with last week-end—couldn't it? Unless . . . 'Why me, Nikolai? I mean, what—what do you envisage, exactly?'

'I envisage a good life together, Janine. I think we could make a good marriage . . .'

She did not interrupt him as he continued. He put to her what he considered a very good case for marriage—and she felt as if she were slowly dying. He sounded just like Michael Granger, telling her how much they had in common, except for one difference: at least Michael professed to love her. But love did not enter into Nikolai's thinking, of course. To him, it was not a necessary ingredient for a successful marriage.

'. . . I'm aware of the difference in our ages,' he went on, 'but I think that's acceptable in our case. I mean, you're not a teenager. You're twenty-three, mature enough to take a step like this and be sure of what you're doing, fully aware of the responsibilities involved in marriage.

'Paris can offer you just as much as London, but you're well aware of that. If you want night life, the high life, we'd need only to go to Paris. We could spend our week-ends there. How much time I put in at the factory is entirely up to me, as you know, so if you'd rather spend half your time in the city and half in the country—well, that would be fine by me. And we could travel, wherever in the world you like. We could have it all, the world at our fingertips.'

He looked at her expectantly. He had finished putting his case and he was waiting for an answer. Janine became aware that her fingernails were digging into the palms of her hands. She released them, picked up her wine and finished it. It was pride alone which enabled her to keep her composure. 'Is that it? And this is your recipe for a successful marriage? The answer is no, Nikolai.'

She was hurting terribly, and it didn't help when he covered her hand with his, 'No, darling, that isn't quite all of it. I—in you I've found what's missing from my life. I've missed you these past two weeks.'

He had missed her? Was that *all*? And he thought that was a good enough reason to marry her? She laughed it off; it was the only way she could possibly cope with this! 'Sorry, Nikolai, but marriage is not included in my plans.'

He was watching her closely, his fingers tightening around hers. 'Is there anything you can add to that?'

Anger shot through her suddenly. She pulled her hand away, almost hating him in that instant for that too-practical mind of his. She was about to snap at him, but she caught hold of her emotions just in time, knowing that if he saw how he was hurting her, he might guess what she was really feeling. So it was coolly that she brought up the question of Michelle Duval. 'Lara showed me your photograph in the newspaper last Sunday,' she said, with a manufactured smile, 'and I'll say this for you—you're the first man I've known who has dated one woman one week-end and then proposed to another a week later! Really, Nikolai! And you tell me you've missed me?'

He was not at all put out. 'What the devil . . .? You mean Michelle? But that was business!'

'Oh, yes?' she laughed.

'Oh, yes,' he echoed seriously. 'Well, maybe I should say it was indirectly business. I've known Michelle for quite a time—through her father. I do business with his bank, and he's a friend. Michelle's fiancé broke off their engagement a few weeks ago and she'd been so depressed that her father was getting seriously worried about her. He rang me and asked me to take her out for the evening.'

Lightly, she said, 'You say that as if it were a hardship.'

'Not at all,' he admitted. 'I enjoyed the evening. We both did.'

How typical of him! He never said what he didn't mean, nor had he ever lied to her. Again she had to admire his honesty. Dear God, if only that other thing were not lacking in him, that other thing which was so vital to his completeness as a person—*if only he could love her!*

'Janine? Will you think about it, my proposal?'

She looked at him steadily, completely composed. 'No, Nikolai, I won't think about it. The answer is no.' Beyond the cool façade she was weeping inwardly at the irony of the situation. His asking her to marry him had been beyond her wildest hopes; she had known from the start that there was no chance of his falling in love with her. With her or any other woman, for that matter. It just wasn't in his emotional make-up. And here he was, proposing to her, and she had to refuse because she would never, ever, marry in such circumstances.

But the trauma was not over yet. Nikolai was considering her in silence, his eyes narrowed slightly. 'I was about to ask you for your reasons, Janine, but I've worked it out for myself. Maybe I should have known better than to ask you. You won't marry me because you're not in love with me. You see, I remember that for you this is a necessary ingredient. I suppose you're thinking you might just as well marry Granger as marry me.'

'Precisely,' she said, turning her attention to the waiter who was approaching with the sweet trolley.

Things did not get easier for her, even though Nikolai changed the subject at that point and he did not bring up the suggestion of marriage again. For that, she was grateful, but the hurt inside her did not lessen as the evening wore on. It was as if . . . as if he had offered her a job, which she had refused, and he was unperturbed. He was as unperturbed as a prospective employer

would be. But then why shouldn't he be? If he
wanted to settle down, if he thought it time he
acquired himself a wife, then he could make his offer
to another suitable candidate. He wouldn't have to
ask often before he got an acceptance, that was for
sure!

He kissed her when they pulled up at the back of her
parents' house a couple of hours later. All the lights
were on downstairs, which meant that Rose and Archie
were still up, which meant that her time in private with
Nikolai had come to an end.

Nikolai switched the car lights off and took hold of
her roughly, suddenly, his mouth claiming hers in a way
which was almost brutal. But she did not resist him; she
couldn't. The feel of his lips on hers was something she
never had been able to resist.

And even now, in a kiss which seemed to have anger
behind it rather than passion, she responded eagerly.
But the kiss changed suddenly, from anger to hunger,
suddenly and unmistakably ... Nikolai's hands moved
from her back to her breasts and she stiffened. 'Nikolai,
no! Please don't——'

But he didn't hear her, or he ignored her protest. He
was caressing her breasts, and a low moan sounded in
his throat as one hand moved to her thigh, beneath her
skirt.

'Nikolai, stop that!' She did not consider herself safe;
he had once come to her bedroom in the early hours of
the morning, what if ... 'Damn you, Nikolai, leave me
alone!' She pulled away from him and flung the car
door open, but he caught hold of her by the wrist,
forcing her to stay in her seat.

'Janine, you're driving me *crazy*. You won't marry
me, you won't let me make love to you—what the hell
am I going to do about you? What do you want of me,
for God's sake?'

She closed her eyes against his anger. This was her
fault—why did he have the power to bring out such a
response in her when she was in his arms? Why had she
allowed herself to return his kiss when she knew full
well she would be asking for trouble?

'Just friendship,' she lied. 'That's all I ever wanted of you, Nikolai.'

He let go of her at once, and only then did she look at him. This time it was he who broke the contact of their eyes. He got out of the car and slammed the door, moving round to the passenger side to take hold of her arm in a grip which was painful.

She gasped. 'What the devil's the matter with you? You're hurting me!'

'You!' he snapped, glancing at her furiously as he marched her to the back door of the house. 'And you're hurting me—in a way you know nothing about!'

She blushed at the implication, but she did not apologise. He knew the score, so why the hell didn't he just keep his hands *off* her!

CHAPTER ELEVEN

JANINE's first few days in London were spent shopping in the West End. She had brought from Jersey her car, her clothes, her hi-fi and record collection, but she needed a new hairdryer, a few personal items and some bedlinen.

Pauline's flat was in Ealing, West London, within walking distance of South Ealing tube station. It was a first floor flat in an old, converted house in a fairly quiet and respectable road, but it was a little drab despite Pauline's efforts to brighten the place up with plants and lamps and colourful paintings.

So far, Janine was not exactly enchanted with London. She had visited her friend here several times in the past, of course, but living here was another matter. Compared to the Channel Islands the city was dusty and dirty, but she thought that the drabness of her new home might be contributing to her disenchantment. And, so far, nothing she had seen or done had served as a distraction from the man who was constantly on her mind, even invading her dreams.

In Jersey, on the day after Nikolai's proposal, during the hours she had spent with Pauline she had told her old friend every last detail of her relationship with Nikolai—from the evening she had met him in Lille to her refusal of his cold-blooded suggestion of marriage.

'Too right!' Pauline had said scathingly. 'Thank God you refused him! He must be pretty desperate to have you if he went as far as offering marriage!'

'Quite.' Janine smiled thinly. 'I'm not suffering from any illusions, Pauline, don't worry about that.'

'I'm glad to hear it.' Pauline's voice had held a note of warning. 'And make sure you don't start kidding yourself if he contacts you in the future.'

'He won't.'

'He might. You're a challenge to him, Jan. A sexual challenge.' Pauline was puffing at a cigarette, thoughtful, half-sprawled on the settee in her parents' living room. She was several inches shorter than Janine, a vivacious redhead with a strong personality, a little thin but attractive with it.

She swung her legs to the floor and reached for the ashtray. 'All men are selfish, and Garth was the biggest bastard of them all!' She was referring to the Islander to whom she had been engaged two years ago, engaged and subsequently jilted by. 'He was the first man to make love to me, *after* we got engaged, and what happened? We were lovers for six months and then he tells me he feels he's not ready for marriage after all, that he's emigrating to South Africa because he's been offered a good job!'

She threw up her hands, still angry at the memory. 'Men! I just wish I could live without them, but I have my—needs—like anyone else. As for your fellow, Nikolai, all he was offering you was a permanent sexual relationship.'

Janine nodded thoughtfully. 'I—I suppose so . . . Maybe I should feel flattered,' she added bitterly, 'since he didn't know what he would be getting.'

'He had a good idea,' Pauline said coldly. 'That's all your relationship was based on—physical attraction.'

To that, Janine had said nothing. But she knew

Pauline was *wrong* there. There had been far more to her relationship with Nikolai than their physical attraction . . .

Now, however, as she let herself into the flat, loaded down with her shopping, she wondered about that. It had been three weeks since she had seen Nikolai. She had worked another two weeks in the travel agency after he had left at Easter, and she had been in London almost a week, but she had not heard from him, not a word.

To say that she missed him would not begin to describe the feeling of emptiness inside her. She put her shopping in her bedroom, kicked off her shoes and headed for the kitchen, in search of a cold drink.

The best thing to do would be to keep herself busy. She didn't need to start work straight away; she had savings to fall back on and she knew she could always ask her father for money if necessary, but it would be better for her to be busy. Finding work as a temp was no problem; she had already registered with an employment agency and had been told that for one with her skills in shorthand and typing, work was readily available, that she could start any time. Finding the right permanent job might be a little difficult, but she would cross that bridge when she was ready to.

'This place needs decorating.' Janine made the announcement when she had lived with Pauline for exactly one week.

'Tell me something new.' Pauline was sitting on the settee, putting on her make-up while Janine ate her dinner at the table. She was going out for a meal with a man called Alex, someone she had met through her work as a secretary in a large company of solicitors.

He was a pleasant man, Janine thought. Pauline had been out with him twice before and had introduced him to Janine when he called for her on their second date.

It was Sunday today, a wet Sunday. The rain was trickling steadily down the windows and Janine was looking at it, telling herself off for feeling so . . . so flat. Here she was in the swinging city; she should make an

effort to go out herself this evening. But she wouldn't.
There was nowhere she could think of where it would
be appropriate for her to go alone. Except, perhaps, the
cinema. 'Sorry, Pauline, what did you say?'

'I said we could have the flat decorated. I can afford
it now I'm only paying half the rent.'

Janine brightened. 'We can do it ourselves!'

This was met with a grimace. 'No, thanks! I haven't
got either the inclination or the first clue about
decorating.'

'But I have! I helped Dad many times when I was a
teenager.'

'Then help yourself! Since you're saving me money
on labour, I'll pay for the paint and stuff and you do
the work. How's that?'

'Fair enough.' Janine was actually looking forward to
it. 'I wish the shops were open today, I want to start
now!'

Pauline looked heavenward.

'I was going to ring the agency tomorrow morning
and tell them I'm ready to start work,' Janine went on,
'but I'll skip this week and decorate this room instead—
and the bathroom! Now, what about choosing the
paper, the colour of the paint?'

'Meet me in my lunch hour tomorrow and we'll sort
something out. Are you *sure* you want to do this?'

Janine thought about that question the following
night, when it was too late. She had bitten off more
than she could chew, she suspected, looking at the
daunting amount of paper, paint and paraphernalia she
and Pauline had bought.

She started there and then, tackling the living room
first. Pauline was home, but she kept out of the way,
making it quite plain that she would not get involved.
By Tuesday afternoon she had finished the painting
part of the job, and by Wednesday lunch time she was
actually hanging paper when Pauline phoned to say she
would be going out with Alex straight from work. The
interruption resulted in the first strip of paper she had
to throw away—having put her foot through it when
she'd scrabbled down the ladder to answer the phone!

She surveyed her day's work before making her dinner that evening, a little uncertain, now, about the paper they had chosen but fairly satisfied with her workmanship. She tested her back for aches; not too bad! After dinner she would take a hot bath and then start again.

But the doorbell rang just as she started peeling potatoes. Because the ring was at the door of the flat and not the outer door, the door to the house, Janine thought it must be one of her neighbours. She stopped what she was doing, thinking it odd because she hardly knew them.

It happened just as she reached the door ... quite suddenly she was consumed by a feeling of—something very hard to describe. The feeling did not alarm her, because it was not the first time she had experienced it. She knew, then, who had rung her door bell.

He was smiling, his indigo eyes telling her he was pleased to see her. Tall and imposing in a dark business suit, he looked more attractive than ever. His black hair had been damped by the drizzle outside and was even more curly because of it, cut close to his skull in that way that accentuated the lean planes of his face.

Janine's stomach contracted so violently that she felt as if she had been kicked there. It was so strange, being shocked and yet not surprised at seeing him. She spoke quickly, managing to put lightness into her voice simply because she had to, she did not want him to know the effect this was having on her. 'Well! This is a surprise! And what brings you to the big, bad city?'

'Is it?' He laughed, bending to kiss her cheeks. 'Business. I didn't know I was coming here until this morning. I phoned Lara and got your address, thinking I'd take a chance on finding you in ... and hoping you'd be free for dinner this evening.'

Acutely selfconscious because she looked a wreck, she pushed back the loose strands of hair which had escaped from her ponytail clip. 'I—well, actually I was just——'

'Is this a new fashion?' Nikolai was examining her face carefully, and she hardly knew what to do with herself.

'I—I'm up to my eyes decorating. I'm afraid——'

'Literally,' he interrupted, tapping her on the nose with a finger. 'You've got splashes of paste on your nose, your cheeks and your eyebrows!' He laughed outrageously, and Janine joined in. It was by far the easiest thing to do!

Suddenly his arms were around her, their laughter dying away. 'I've missed you, Janine,' he said softly, looking into her eyes.

She couldn't speak, her heart was hammering so fast that she could hardly breathe. Had he really missed her? Oh, not half as much as she had missed him! And she didn't have the strength to move away from him, she was too pleased, desperately pleased, to see him, to feel his arms around her.

But her mind was telling her that she must not take seriously what he had said, that he had come to London on business and was merely calling to see her because he happened to be in town. She moved away from him then, briskly. 'How long are you in London for, Nikolai?'

'Just for tonight. I——' He caught hold of her wrist as she turned from him, pulling her around so he could see her face properly. 'I am here on business, Janine, but I don't need that or any other excuse for coming to see you. Do I?'

Janine sighed inwardly, wishing she had the strength to tell him to go away. That was what she wanted to do. Seeing him was disturbing her to an extent he would not begin to understand.

'Do I?'

'No.' Coward that she was, it was more than she could do to send him packing. 'Of course not,' she added lightly. 'You're one of the family, after all.'

'So you are going to ask me in—eventually?' he grinned.

'Of course!' She motioned him towards the living room, trying desperately to calm down inwardly, to behave naturally.

'*Mon Dieu*, what a mess!'

'What did you expect?' she asked, seeing his look of

horror as he turned to face her. 'I'm decorating. I told you!'

'And who's helping you?'

'No one. I'm doing——' She broke off, indignant. Nikolai was roaring with laughter and she couldn't see the joke. 'What's so funny? What is it?'

It was quite a time before he sobered, pointing to the wall. 'Is that a new fashion, too?' He flung aside one of the sheets she had used to cover the settee and sat down. 'My dear girl, go and take a bath and get dressed up. I'm taking you somewhere glamorous for dinner. I think you've earned it!' Again he exploded with laughter. He was pointing to the wall she had just finished, trying very hard to control himself. 'That paper! Look! Look at it!'

Janine looked at it. True, she had liked it better on the roll than she did now, but it wasn't that bad! 'Well, I like it and Pauline likes it. It's——' It was only then that she saw what she'd done. The pattern on the paper was a quiet one, a series of faint lines with a tiny motif between them—and the strip in the centre of the wall was on upside down.

She squealed in horror, shifting her hands from her hips to her lower back—which had suddenly started aching! 'Oh, *bother*! No wonder I thought it didn't look as it should! Talk about not seeing the wood for the— do you know, I kept thinking it didn't look quite right?'

If she could have seen the expression on her own face as she turned to Nikolai, she would have started laughing sooner than she did. As it was, there were a few seconds during which she silently gave vent to her disappointment and frustration by swearing inwardly. It was his fresh bout of laughter that set her off . . . she laughed until there were tears on her lashes, until her stomach was aching with it.

She did as he told her to. She bathed and dressed up and admitted to herself that it was lovely to be handing herself over to Nikolai for the evening, for that was what it felt like. He phoned for a taxi, poured her a brandy, which she drank while they waited for the taxi to come, then he took her by the hand and off they went.

CHAPTER TWELVE

'YOU'RE *nuts*!' Pauline was reading the riot act while hurriedly eating bacon and eggs the following morning. 'And I warned you, didn't I?'

Janine didn't eat breakfast. She was sipping at a cup of tea, riddled with misgivings at what she had done. Last night, on delivering her safely to her front door, Nikolai had announced that he was going to stay in London and help her to finish the decorating ... and she had accepted the offer.

He had booked in at the airport hotel for the one night he had planned on staying and this morning, he'd said, he would move to a local hotel in Ealing. He had told her to expect him around eleven o'clock—and not to start work before he arrived.

'How long is he staying?' Pauline wanted to know.

'Till Sunday.'

'Oh, *Jan*! What's *wrong* with you? You're not thinking straight! Can't you see that you'd have saved yourself a lot of hassle—and heartache—if you'd given him the brush-off? You should never have let him in! I mean what point, what *point* was there in leaving Jersey to avoid his visits there, when you're encouraging him to spend time with you here?'

'But I—I didn't know he came to London on business. He—he comes often, but ... oh, what's the use? I just didn't have the strength to send him away. Seeing him, being with him, makes me feel so ... I don't know how to describe it. I'm not whole unless I'm with him. I——'

'I know.' Pauline's voice was quiet now. 'I know all about it, kiddo, I felt like that about Garth.' Bitterly she added, 'And look how much good it's done me.' She pushed her plate away. 'I'm running late, will you wash up for me, Jan?'

Janine nodded, looking at her helplessly. 'I know

170

you're right. I know you're only thinking of me, but I ... I love him, Pauline.'

Her friend sighed, long and hard. 'I know you do, you poor devil!' And with that she went to work, leaving Janine mulling everything over in her mind.

Of course Pauline was right, and how like her it was to be absolutely blunt. It was one of the things Janine could rely on, one of the reasons she loved Pauline. She was a good friend and she pulled no punches. She was also a living demonstration of the fact that running away didn't always help in affairs of the heart. It was almost two years since Garth had called off their wedding plans and she had not had a relationship which lasted more than a few weeks with any man since. She, too, had travelled the road to nowhere, just as Janine was doing now ...

It was almost eight-fifteen. She could go to the hotel Nikolai was booking into this morning and meet him when he arrived, tell him to get out of her life, to leave her alone. He would know, if she did that, how she felt about him, and he would laugh at her. But wouldn't that be better than this ... this one-way ticket to disillusionment?

No, she wasn't actually under any illusions. She was doing what she was doing with her eyes wide open, and furthermore she was aware that Nikolai was determined to make love to her. As Pauline had said, he must be pretty desperate if he went as far as offering marriage ... That was what it was all about, this visit of his. Janine didn't think for one minute that he would concentrate only on decorating for the next four days.

She put her head in her hands, knowing full well that she wouldn't, couldn't, tell him to get out of her life. She was not that strong. As for her ability to continue resisting him physically ... well, she doubted whether she would have that kind of strength, either.

But Janine's strength in that respect was not tested during the next few days. Indeed, Nikolai seemed to avoid anything but the most casual of physical contact.

The days were, in fact, full of laughter, because while Nikolai was undoubtedly a wizard when it came to engineering, he proved to be as good at decorating as Janine was! In the kitchen, however, he surprised her. It was he who prepared their lunches, she who did the washing up.

During the evenings he took her in to the West End, to the theatre, to long and leisurely dinners in expensive restaurants. And these evenings were ended with brief, goodnight kisses at her front door, kisses which could only be described as chaste.

She started work as a temp on the following Monday afternoon, the day after Nikolai left for France, and he phoned her during the evening. He phoned also on Tuesday evening and on Wednesday ... to make arrangements to see her at the week-end.

'That's it, then.' Pauline spoke decisively as Janine put down the telephone receiver, having heard Janine's side of the telephone call.

'What do you mean?' Janine looked at her uncertainly.

'I mean he's going through the courting routine.'

'Courting routine?'

'Come off it, Jan, you're not that naïve.' Pauline was sitting on the sofa, her legs curled under her. 'This is the start of *the wearing down process*. Remember what I told you in Jersey? Don't start kidding yourself. Well, I was right. You're a challenge to him, Jan—a sexual challenge. And having met him I can only say I wouldn't blame you in the least if you do have an affair with him. He *is* something else, I can't deny it! In fact, maybe it would be better for you to "get on with it", to quote your own words. ...'

Thoughtful, Janine was sitting with her chin propped up in her hands. 'Having an affair with a man, any man, is not something I can just *decide* to do!'

'Ha! You don't have to. Nikolai has already made the decision for you.'

'But—he made no attempt ... He didn't lay a finger on me last week-end.'

'Of course he didn't.' Pauline smiled, adopting an attitude of patience. 'He's got too much finesse, sophistication—and all those years of experience. And you? You're a mere babe by comparison. He knows precisely what to do to wear you down, he'll be attentive, he'll get you to trust him, he'll wine you and dine you and then—bingo! You'll find yourself in bed with him. And as I say, I wouldn't blame you in the least.'

Janine leaned tiredly against the cushions of the armchair, grateful that she had Pauline to help her keep a balanced, objective view of things. She was right in what she'd said. Nikolai was not a man to resist a challenge. Pauline had only confirmed what Janine already knew, deep down inside. So why had she been fool enough to think that maybe, just maybe she would be the woman Nikolai finally fell for? There was nothing special about her. She was attractive but she was not beautiful, in spite of what he'd told her. But then lavish compliments such as that were no doubt part and parcel of the wearing down process, as Pauline had called it.

She got to her feet. 'I—think I'll take a bath and have an early night.'

'I've upset you.' Pauline looked worried now.

'No, no, honestly. You've only confirmed what I already know. I'm my own worst enemy. But I'm on this merry-go-round and I can't get off. I don't even want to.'

She gave Pauline a hug. 'Goodnight, and thanks for being such a good friend.'

Pauline shrugged. 'I'll give it a month. After all, it's just as easy for him to travel to London for his week-ends as it is for him to visit his girl-friends in Paris. *One month*, Jan, and you'll be lovers.'

One month later it was the end of May, the Bank Holiday week-end. Janine and Nikolai were on Jersey for the party which Robbie and Lara were giving to celebrate the opening of their restaurant.

There had been an unfortunate and expensive hitch in the conversion work on the premises, in the form of a gas explosion which had caused a lot of damage in the kitchens. Fortunately it had happened during the night, so nobody had been hurt, and the work was finished now.

It was Saturday night, and the restaurant was due to open on Monday. All Robbie's friends were present including, of course, Michael Granger. Michael had brought his new fiancée with him to the party—Suzie Smythe.

During the evening, Janine caught herself looking at both Suzie and Michael often, smiling to herself because she had been right all along in thinking that Michael was not really in love with her. There was a man who really had suffered from an illusion. If he had really loved Janine, he would not be engaged to someone else only two months after she had walked out of his life. Any more than Pauline would have got engaged to someone after Garth had walked out of her life, any more than Janine would get engaged to someone when her relationship with Nikolai was over.

Relationship. That was still the right word. She could not call it an affair, because Pauline's prophecy had been wrong. One month had passed, and she and Nikolai were not lovers, although his kisses of late had been far from chaste. But he had kept his passion in check, and Janine knew better than to encourage him . . .

'Are you having regrets?'

She turned to find Nikolai standing close behind her. The tables of the restaurant had been moved to one side now that the meal was over, a superb meal which had been supervised by Robbie, and people were dancing, chatting, circulating.

In the subdued lighting of the restaurant his skin looked even darker than usual, contrasted as it was against the whiteness of his dress shirt. Everyone had dressed up for this occasion, in response to Robbie's instructions, and the evening was going beautifully.

'About what?'

Nikolai was not only unsmiling, he looked annoyed. 'About Michael Granger, of course.'

'Don't be silly! I told you I never——'

'I know what you told me. But you've spent half the evening looking in his direction.'

'And Suzie's,' she pointed out. 'To tell you the truth I'm wondering what the future holds in store for them. It's obvious how Suzie feels, but I'm wondering what Michael feels for her, actually.'

'You mean he might be marrying her on the rebound.'

'No, that isn't what I meant. Michael never loved me, Nikolai. I can tell you——'

'You can tell me what you like,' he said crisply, his eyes troubled as he examined her face. 'But you're no expert on these matters. I wonder how much you actually know about love? It seems you can't recognise it when it's staring you in the face.'

She shrugged. 'Then tell me what you think about them.'

'I have no opinion on the subject of those two. I have other things to think about, my own troubles to contend with.'

And with that he excused himself and invited Rose to dance.

Janine was staring after him, confused, when Lara came up to her and asked the very question which was going through her mind. 'Janine, what's wrong with Nikolai tonight? He's—remote. Suddenly he's—you know, the way he used to be before he met you. And only this afternoon I was thinking how much good you've been doing him these past few weeks. He's spent every week-end with you, hasn't he?'

'Yes. Well,' Janine amended hastily, 'he's spent every week-end in a *hotel*, Lara.'

Lara smiled. She looked at Janine for a long moment, and there was no amusement in the blue eyes which were usually sparkling with laughter. 'What a pity. I'm very, very sorry to hear that.'

Astonished, Janine opened her mouth to speak, but Lara had walked away. It seemed that her first week-end at home was provoking people to make all sorts of cryptic remarks to her. She had had several remarks from her parents about her relationship with Nikolai, just odd little comments about how nice it was that they were getting on so well together.

Things came to a head on the following week-end, in London. Nikolai had asked her several times if she would go to him for a few days, to his chateau in Lille, but she didn't want to do that because she felt safer with him in the flat, mainly because Pauline was there most of the time—and always late at night.

But during the first week-end of June, Pauline wasn't around. She told Janine on the Friday morning that she was going away with Alex for the week-end, that he was 'growing' on her and she had decided to sleep with him. How she could simply make up her mind to sleep with a man towards whom her feelings were so—so lukewarm, Janine didn't know. But some people were like that, and who was to say if it were wrong? One must live and let live.

And didn't Nikolai have the same attitude? With him it would be sex for the sake of sex, sex without love. But that was not for Janine. That would, to her, be as tasteless as marriage without love.

The trouble was that while he did not love her, she was finding it harder and harder to keep to her principles. Because she loved him more and more as time passed.

Nikolai was relaxed and smiling when he arrived around nine o'clock on the Friday evening, which was a little later than the time he usually arrived. But he had told Janine over the phone what time he would get to the flat, and she had prepared their dinner, a traditional *bouillabaisse*. With appropriate French wine it went down very well indeed, and there was no sign of the dark mood which had descended upon him so suddenly during the previous week-end. On the contrary, he was making her laugh, teasing her.

'So!' he said, after praising her efforts in the kitchen, 'I can spend the night in Pauline's bed, can I? Could have saved money on a hotel this week-end . . .'

'I'm not sure Pauline would like that idea. I'm not sure I do!'

He stretched out on the settee, looking at her blankly. 'Why not? You've got plenty of spare bed linen, haven't you?'

'Yes.' Janine had just finished clearing the table and she flopped into an armchair. It was a warm, lovely evening and for once she was going to leave the washing up till the morning.

'But you'd feel threatened if you were alone with me here in the flat? Even in separate rooms?'

'Yes,' she grinned. 'Aren't you going to drink your coffee? It's going cold.'

'Don't change the subject. Do you know what I feel like doing tonight?'

'Yes,' she said again. 'But I think we'll go for a walk instead!'

He smiled at her the indigo eyes sparkling wickedly. 'But Pauline won't be back tonight, and while I'm in no mood for walking . . .'

Janine got up and poured him a brandy, which he always enjoyed after a meal. She also switched the television on because neither of them were in the mood to go out, and the distraction of the box might put an end to a conversation with was making her heart jump all over the show in a mixture of nervousness and excitement.

It put an end to conversation altogether. There was a political debate going on, and Nikolai got caught up in it. He switched off the overhead light, stretched out on the settee again and lit a cheroot. But Janine was watching him far more than she was watching the television. Dear God, he was beautiful! In a black, open neck shirt and close-fitting corduroy slacks she could see every contour of his body as he lay, the depth of his magnificent chest, the hard, muscular thighs. . . .

Her eyes travelled back to his face, only to find that he was watching her, watching him. He touched a button on the control box and the television screen went blank, leaving the room a little darker, and in a silence which spoke volumes . . .

He got up, not taking his eyes from hers as he took hold of both her wrists, pulling her to her feet. And then she was in his arms and his mouth claimed hers with none of the tenderness she knew he was capable of. The tenderness came when she stopped making what was only a token resistance, when she yielded to the sheer pleasure of his kiss. She slid her arms around the hard strength of his back, her breasts straining against his chest as their embrace tightened. His arousal was immediate, shocking to her as the length of his body pressed against her own. Shocking, but more than she could resist . . .

Nikolai lifted her bodily, scooping her high into his arms as he carried her to her bedroom, kissing her even as he walked, as he laid her down on her bed.

Janine was slipping into a dark vortex of desire, that state where her rational mind and her body seemed to separate. Just as it had happened that night in Lille, so long ago, she seemed to be looking on, hearing the protests of her common sense even as she arched towards him. She could hear Pauline's voice, too, haunting her from some dim recess of her mind, telling her that she had lost, that Nikolai had won . . .

The voice faded, and Janine's fingers were in the short, crisp curls on Nikolai's hair, her lips exploring the base of his throat, spurring him on even as she knew this was the beginning of the end for her.

And then it was Nikolai's voice she was hearing, but this voice was real, and it was telling her with irresistible eroticism what he wanted to do to her, how he wanted to make love to her. No man had ever spoken to her like that, with such detail, yet without the slightest hint of crudity. Coming from Nikolai, his voice a warm breeze against her ear, it was poetic and sensual in the extreme.

And she loved it.

She was not even aware that he had opened the buttons of her blouse. She was aware, then, of nothing but the images he was weaving for her with his words. Those, and her unspoken compliance.

Then his hands slid on to the silkiness of her breasts, cupping them gently, squeezing sensually, slowly. Oh, so slowly he caressed her, kissing her mouth as his hands explored her, taking her taut nipples between finger and thumb and pulling gently, tauntingly.

Janine's hands were moving along the hard muscles of his back, beneath the material of his shirt, bringing forth from him a deep groan of pleasure which in turn sent her blood pounding through her veins. And all the time his mouth was making love to her independently, phis tongue robing the moist warmth of her mouth in an erotic appetiser of what was to come when he claimed her body with his own.

The Frenchman's kiss tamed her into submission while at the same time it lifted her to dizzying heights of arousal. She was passive now, clinging to him as her legs twined themselves around his legs in invitation, as her body arched against him.

But they were still fully clothed, and in the seconds when he took his mouth from hers, pushing the blouse, her bra straps from her shoulders and reaching for the buttons of his shirt, the voices in her head came back with a vengeance. She stilled his hands, her own hands shaking as she spoke without looking at him. 'Nikolai, I—I can't.'

In answer he slid his fingers into her hair and claimed her mouth with an ardour she had only glimpsed before, and she panicked because he was leaving her no choice, because he would brook no argument this time. She wrenched her head away, gasping for air as her heart seemed to move up into her throat. 'Nikolai, don't! *Please!*'

'Janine——' His voice was thick with arousal. 'Darling, for God's sake——' He wasn't angry. He just didn't believe what she was telling him.

'I can't—I can't. I *can't*!' A sob escaped from her as her vision blurred with the threat of tears. She was cursing herself for her weakness, mental and physical, and she was cursing him for the slow and insidious expertise he had used in bringing her to this pitch of excitement. Not just tonight, but during the past few weeks.

Oh, how right Pauline had been in her prediction! How right, almost to the day! He had lulled her into a false sense of security, and now . . .

'Get away from me, Nikolai. Get out of my room—out of my life!'

'*What?*' Now he was angry—dear God, he was angry! 'What the devil is the matter with you, woman?' He was staring at her in disbelief. He took hold of her shoulders and shook her—hard. 'Janine, I want to marry you, to *marry* you. What's happening here? I'm talking about a lifelong commitment and you're telling me to get out of your life?'

She pulled away from him, yanking a pillow in front of her as if it would serve as a means of protection. 'You're not talking about *commitment*!' she exploded. 'You're just talking about a permanent sexual relationship!'

She saw him grow pale beneath the darkness of his skin, she saw his face, the lines of his mouth tightening in anger and distaste. He was standing now, and very quietly he said, 'I never thought I'd hear such vulgarity from your lips, Janine. I want to marry you, I want you as I've never wanted——'

'From me?' she shouted. 'Vulgarity from *me*?' What did he think his proposal had been if not the very essence of cold-blooded calculation? What could be more vulgar than that? To her, nothing. 'Yes, you want to marry me—for all the wrong reasons! You want me, full stop!'

'I think the best thing I can do is leave you to cool off.' He was tucking his shirt back into his slacks, his voice cold with fury. 'I don't know who's been whispering down your ear lately, but at a guess I'd say it's that aggressive flatmate of yours.'

'What? How dare you talk of her——'

'Didn't you hear me? I said it's that bitter and twisted redhead you live with. The hard-bitten bitch you call your friend.'

Furious, Janine threw the pillow at him—a futile and impotent gesture. 'Get out of here! It's *over*, Nikolai. From now on you'd better spend your week-ends the way you used to spend them—doing your sexual exercises with your mistresses!'

He didn't even answer that one. He just walked out of the room and closed the door quietly behind him.

Janine was hysterical with anger, hurt, with love for him and hatred of him. 'Well, what difference does it make?' she screamed through the closed door. 'What difference whether you have your fun in London or in Paris? It's all the same to you!'

The outer door of the flat slammed shut so hard that the whole house shook, and Janine sat, staring blindly at nothing.

CHAPTER THIRTEEN

SHE almost ran after him.

She wanted to run after him, to lean against the hard strength of his body and unburden herself of all the love she felt for him, all the love which was locked up inside her. All the love she had never dared to express.

She dropped her head into her hands, crying noisily. What had been the matter with her tonight? Nikolai had been right to wonder. She couldn't credit her own behaviour, couldn't explain it even to herself. What had caused her violent and uncharacteristic reaction?

At length she went into the living room and drank a glass of brandy, just one. It was as if, tonight, all her emotions had ganged up on her and exploded. And Nikolai had taken the brunt of the explosion . . .

Heavens above, she had shrieked at him like a fishwife! He must think her insane. This, when the past few weeks had been so beautiful, when they had been such fast and loving friends——

It was a sobering thought, a shocking, sobering thought. Loving?

The wearing down process. There was Pauline's voice again. And Nikolai had spoken so scathingly of her! He never said what he didn't mean, and he had spoken of her so viciously all of a sudden.

She had never asked him what he thought of Pauline and of course he would not volunteer what was going through his mind, especially when Janine was so obviously fond of the girl.

She went into the kitchen and tackled the washing up like an automaton, unable to sit still because she was so deeply disturbed, not only because of the row but also because of the doubts which were crowding her mind now, doubts about Pauline.

Pauline had repeated her warnings daily to Janine, telling her both at breakfast and dinner times not to start fooling herself about Nikolai's attentions, his weekly visits. Even when he had sent flowers for her birthday, Pauline had seen an ulterior motive in it, had put it down as part of Nikolai's seduction or 'courting' routine.

Was she bitter, basically set against men, whom she admitted she could not live without, because she was still in love with Garth. No. No, she wasn't in love with Garth. She hated him now, she had once said as much. Or rather, she hated what he had done to her.

And she had been whispering into Janine's ear, constantly, her remarks about Nikolai a steady drip, drip, drip of corrosive acid—and Janine had been receptive to it because she was so insecure to begin with.

She was still insecure. But she had to talk to Nikolai, now, about that she had no doubts at all. She walked quickly into the living room and picked up the phone— and put it down again. She didn't even know the number of the hotel he was staying in. She hunted for the telephone directory and picked up the phone again, only to put it down again as she glanced at her watch. It was three o'clock in the morning; she couldn't ring him at this hour.

She sat, motionless. Oh, Lord, what if he'd already left the hotel? What if he were on his way back to France? She snatched up the receiver and dialled the number of the hotel.

She was connected to Nikolai's room in a flash, her heart pounding with relief because he had not checked out. 'Nikolai? I—were you awake?'

'I haven't gone to bed.' There was no anger in his voice now. It was just—dull.

'I want to talk to you. Now. I—I hurt your feelings tonight and I—I want to apologise. I want to see you.' There followed a lengthy, excruciating silence. 'Nikolai? Nikolai!'

He spoke quietly, so quietly that she had to strain to hear him. 'To apologise? So you do care that much? You care enough to be concerned about hurting me?'

Care? Care! Oh, if only he knew! But how could he, why should he, when she had never dared to tell him for fear of . . . for fear of being laughed at. 'Yes, I care. I care, Nikolai!'

There was another, awful, drawn-out silence. 'Do you realise that this is the first time you have ever telephoned me, Janine? Do you? Do you realise that this is the first time you've ever actually told me you *want* to see me? You've always refused to come to me. Will you come to me now? Will *you* come to *me*?'

'Yes. Yes!' He was staying at a hotel near the Common; it was too far to walk, so she told him hastily that she would ring for a taxi.

'Then stay where you are,' he said. 'All I wanted was your willingness. Stay where you are and I'll be right over. I don't want you roaming the streets at this time of night.'

Janine put down the receiver and waited for him. It was the longest half hour of her life.

There was the black shadow of a beard on his face, the tension and tiredness in his face telling of his need for sleep, and yet the deep blue eyes were alert and bright with . . . *tenderness!* He was scanning her face, looking for a response in her eyes, and she walked into his arms as he stepped inside the small hallway of the flat, resting her head against his shoulder while they stood for several seconds in silence.

Nothing was said until they were in the living room. They stood apart then, facing each other, and it was Janine who spoke first. 'You—you wondered . . . you doubted that I cared,' she whispered. 'It's more than that, much more.' She lifted her chin, her body rigid with tension. 'I love you and I'm very much in love with you.'

She saw him change before her eyes, she saw the strangest expression on his face, she heard his sharp intake of breath and his long exhalation. His eyes closed fleetingly, as if of their own volition.

Nikolai wasn't laughing—far from it. He looked like a man who had just been given something he had waited a very long time for. It seemed that a whole day went by before he spoke, and when he did it was to ask for a drink.

Janine moved quickly to the table in the corner, feeling as though her life were hanging in the balance. As he sat, she handed him a glass and watched him as he lit a cheroot, willing him to say something. Just—*something*.

Suddenly he was on his feet again, moving restlessly, leaving his drink untouched. She watched him as he stood for several seconds with his back to her, smoking, gathering his thoughts before he turned to face her.

Then the words poured from him in a torrent which was slow but steady, unhesitant, giving Janine the impression that he had planned exactly what he wanted to say. 'When I went to Jersey in March, I went not only to see my sister but to see you. Since meeting you last October, I had been unable to forget you. I'd thought it was purely a physical attraction you held for me. Even as I left Jersey, I thought that. Or I thought I thought it.'

He spoke the last few words on a sigh, shaking his head. 'I see now that I'd been denying, almost fighting against, what I really felt for you. I love you, Janine. I miss you more than I can explain when I'm not with you. I told you I'd missed you when I asked you to marry me. It was the clumsiest of proposals, I know, but I—I've never before told a woman that I love her and I—I couldn't hope that you felt the same. I had no reason to think you did. And I would have felt . . . too vulnerable, telling you. Even foolish. This probably sounds absurd to you, but while it was easy for me to propose, somehow I just couldn't tell you that I love you.'

He leaned on the windowsill, half sitting, half

standing. 'You know, jealousy is an emotion I had never known before meeting you. I first felt it that night when we went to Granger's party and I saw you dancing with him, saw him holding you so possessively. But it was far worse when you couldn't take your eyes off him at Robert's party. I was as jealous as hell then, and I couldn't handle it. I'd had no experience. Nor was I proud of it. I know it's negative, pointless, but that doesn't stop me feeling it.

'I'm jealous even now—of your life here. I worry about you and I miss you every minute I'm not with you. I want you with *me*, always. If you add it all up, Janine, I think you'll see that I mean it when I tell you now that I love you.'

She could do no more than nod dumbly. He had said that to tell her before would have made him feel too vulnerable, even foolish. No, this did not sound in the least absurd to her. How could it when she had refused to tell him of her own feelings for a very similar reason? For fear that he would laugh.

'But there's more to it.' For several seconds the deep blue eyes held hers before he went on. 'And I . . . don't quite know how to describe it, what to call it. I—this is something else I've never experienced before, so I— it's——' He hesitated now, no longer sure of what he wanted to say, searching for the right words.

He switched from English to his native tongue, then back to English as he went on, having difficulty finding the right words in either language. 'It's—something more than just loving you. You're in my thoughts day and night. And I don't just miss you, I . . . being away from you hurts like a physical pain. I can hardly believe this, and it's hard to admit because I feel that I'm not in control of myself. It's like an obsession or an illness. I've lost interest in things, I can't always sleep properly, I can't even concentrate on my work for thinking about you.'

He glanced away from her as he reached for an ashtray, his voice growing quieter and deeper with emotion. 'I feel only half alive without you, like a body without a soul. Yes, I think—I suppose it *is* a kind of illness.' His eyes moved questioningly back to hers. 'Janine? Darling, why are you crying. . .?'

She was crying and then she was laughing, laughing out of pure joy, excitement, incredulity. But it was true! He meant every word he had said to her! He not only loved her, he was *in* love with her! 'Oh, Nikolai! No, it isn't an illness! Darling, come here, come and hold me in your arms while I tell you what it is that's happened to you.'

Nikolai crossed the room swiftly, scooping her high into the air and spinning her around, laughing, nuzzling against her throat as he did so.

'Stop that!' she protested. 'This is a very serious matter!' She fastened her arms around his neck as he set her on her feet, whispering into his ear.

He raised his head to look deeply into her eyes, keeping his arms tightly about her waist. 'But, Janine, I don't believe in that sort of thing!'

She giggled. 'Yes, darling. And let me tell you something else . . .' She was whispering again, kissing his ear between sentences.

'Love at first sight? Oh, Janine, what nonsense! Surely there's no such thing! And I've spent all this time trying to make you love me, trying to make you want——'

'And I've spent all this time hoping you would fall in love with me, thinking it was impossible.' The smile faded from her lips. 'Darling, about Pauline . . . I—I've never told you of her experience with . . . you are right about her, but how did you know? How did you know she'd been getting at me, planting doubts in my mind?'

'I didn't. Well, I know only that I disliked her on sight—I'm sorry, but that's the way it is. Your attitude was always—just that bit different towards me whenever she was present, and tonight you—some of the things you said just didn't sound like you. It wasn't you. I couldn't believe that you doubted me so much that you would accuse me so wrongly.'

'Forgive me, Nikolai. Forgive me for the things I said. I've been under such an emotional strain and I—I just blew up tonight. And darling, please don't think too badly of Pauline. She was hurt once, very badly, and there was no malice in what she's been saying to me about you, really there wasn't. It's just that she thinks *all* men are——'

Nikolai kissed her. He kissed her, and it spoke not only of forgiveness but of his love for her. When she started to move tightly against him, however, he held her at arms' length. 'Go to bed, darling. You get into Pauline's bed and I'll get into yours a little later, in an hour or two. It's very late and we've got a heavy day ahead of us. We'll be flying to Jersey tomorrow and——'

'Pauline's bed?' That was all she had heard. 'Why can't we both get into my bed?'

'Because,' he said firmly, in a voice which was nothing less than businesslike, 'that can wait until after we're married. That way you will have no doubts about me—ever again.'

Janine linked her arms around his neck. 'I have no doubts.'

'You'll get into *Pauline's* bed!' He was laughing, jerking his thumb towards the door, but he meant what he'd said.

She blinked in confusion, realising that he really meant it! 'And—and what are you going to do? Why are you staying up for a while?'

'Because I'm going to ring your mother at daybreak. She'll need all the notice we can give her, she'll have to move quickly with the wedding arrangements, because I intend to marry you before the week is out.' He threw back his head, laughing outrageously. '*Mon Dieu*, they'll be surprised, will they not? All of them! Your parents, Robert and Lara——'

She was laughing, too—at him. 'No. Oh, no, I don't think so!' She put her arms around him tightly, holding him so close that she could feel the beat of his heart. 'My darling Nikolai, I think the only people who'll be surprised when we actually get married will be you and I. Nobody else is as deaf and blind as we have been!'

'But——'

'But nothing. Don't worry about it, my darling! Just take my word for it, and give me a goodnight——'

But the Frenchman was already kissing her.

TAKE THESE 4 Harlequin Romances FREE

Delight in **Mary Wibberley**'s warm romance, MAN OF POWER, the story of a girl whose life changes from drudgery to glamour overnight.....Let THE WINDS OF WINTER by **Sandra Field** take you on a journey of love to Canada's beautiful Maritimes....Thrill to a cruise in the tropics—and a devastating love affair in the aftermath of a shipwreck— in **Rebecca Stratton**'s THE LEO MAN.... Travel to the wilds of Kenya in a quest for love with the determined heroine in **Karen van der Zee**'s LOVE BEYOND REASON.

Harlequin Romances . . . 6 exciting novels published each month! Each month you will get to know interesting, appealing, true-to-life people . . . . You'll be swept to distant lands you've dreamed of visiting . . . . Intrigue, adventure, romance, and the destiny of many lives will thrill you through each Harlequin Romance novel.

Get all the latest books before they're sold out!

As a Harlequin subscriber you actually receive your personal copies of the latest Romances immediately after they come off the press, so you're sure of getting all 6 each month.

Cancel your subscription whenever you wish!

You don't have to buy any minimum number of books. Whenever you decide to stop your subscription just let us know and we'll cancel all further shipments.

Your FREE gift includes

- MAN OF POWER by **Mary Wibberley**
- THE WINDS OF WINTER by **Sandra Field**
- THE LEO MAN by **Rebecca Stratton**
- LOVE BEYOND REASON by **Karen van der Zee**

FREE GIFT CERTIFICATE

and Subscription Reservation

Mail this coupon today!

Harlequin Reader Service

In the U.S.A.	In Canada
2504 West Southern Ave.	P.O. Box 2800, Postal Station A
Tempe, AZ 85282	5170 Yonge Street,
	Willowdale, Ont. M2N 6J3

Please send me my 4 Harlequin Romance novels FREE. Also, reserve a subscription to the 6 NEW Harlequin Romance novels published each month. Each month I will receive 6 NEW Romance novels at the low price of $1.50 each (*Total–$9.00 a month*). There are no shipping and handling or any other hidden charges. I may cancel this arrangement at any time, but even if I do, these first 4 books are still mine to keep. 116 BPR EAVE

NAME	(PLEASE PRINT)

ADDRESS	APT. NO.

CITY

STATE/PROV.	ZIP/POSTAL CODE

This offer is limited to one order per household and not valid to current *Harlequin Romance* subscribers. We reserve the right to exercise discretion in granting membership.

® ™ Trademarks of Harlequin Enterprises Ltd.   R-SUB-2US

If price changes are necessary you will be notified

Enter a uniquely exciting new world with

Harlequin American Romance™

Harlequin American Romances are the first romances to explore today's love relationships. These compelling novels reach into the hearts and minds of women across America... probing the most intimate moments of romance, love and desire.

You'll follow romantic heroines and irresistible men as they boldly face confusing choices. Career first, love later? Love without marriage? Long-distance relationships? All the experiences that make love real are captured in the tender, loving pages of **Harlequin American Romances.**

What makes American women so different when it comes to love? Find out with **Harlequin American Romance!**

Send for your introductory FREE book now!

Get this book FREE!

Harlequin American Romance

Twice in a Lifetime
REBECCA FLANDERS

Mail to:

Harlequin Reader Service

In the U.S.	In Canada
2504 West Southern Ave.	P.O. Box 2800, Postal Station A
Tempe, AZ 85282	5170 Yonge St., Willowdale, Ont. M2N 6J3

YES! I want to be one of the first to discover **Harlequin American Romance.** Send me FREE and without obligation *Twice in a Lifetime*. If you do not hear from me after I have examined my FREE book, please send me the 4 new **Harlequin American Romances** each month as soon as they come off the presses. I understand that I will be billed only $2.25 for each book (total $9.00). There are no shipping or handling charges. There is no minimum number of books that I have to purchase. In fact, I may cancel this arrangement at any time. *Twice in a Lifetime* is mine to keep as a FREE gift, even if I do not buy any additional books.   154 BPA NAZJ

Name	(please print)

Address		Apt. no.

City	State/Prov.	Zip/Postal Code

Signature (if under 18, parent or guardian must sign.)

This offer is limited to one order per household and not valid to current Harlequin American Romance subscribers. We reserve the right to exercise discretion in granting membership. If price changes are necessary, you will be notified.

AMR-SUB-2

Just what the woman on the go needs!

BOOKMATE

The perfect "mate" for all Harlequin paperbacks!

Holds paperbacks open for hands-free reading!

- TRAVELING
- VACATIONING
- AT WORK • IN BED
- COOKING • EATING
- STUDYING

Perfect size for all standard paperbacks, this wonderful invention makes reading a pure pleasure! Ingenious design holds paperback books OPEN and FLAT so even wind can't ruffle pages—leaves your hands free to do other things. Reinforced, wipe-clean vinyl-covered holder flexes to let you turn pages without undoing the strap...supports paperbacks so well, they have the strength of hardcovers!

Snaps closed for easy carrying.

Available now. Send your name, address, and zip or postal code, along with a check or money order for just $4.99 + .75¢ for postage & handling (for a total of $5.74) payable to Harlequin Reader Service to:

Harlequin Reader Service

In the U.S.A.
2504 West Southern Ave.
Tempe, AZ 85282

In Canada
P.O. Box 2800, Postal Station A
5170 Yonge Street,
Willowdale, Ont. M2N 5T5

MATE-1R